HEROES & THIEVES
BOOK ONE
THE NOBLE BANDIT

BY
NICHOLAS M. KROHN

Dedicated to my big brother, Kyle.
Thank you for helping motivate me to complete this
story.
I love you, Bro.

This story pictures many principles, doctrines, and other such aspects from the King James Bible. It is, however, still entertainment and should be treated thusly. Certain specific details from this story do not reflect biblical Christianity or the core beliefs of the author, but were designed for a fictitious world in order to entertain readers. Please use discretion while reading and, should any confusion occur with spiritual principles from this book, you are advised by the author to consult the King James Bible foremost and above this book.

The Zalian Chronicles are a series of stories that reference a number of different cultures in various time-lines through the eyes of an American author. The Zalian Chronicles and the characters within are not meant to symbolize any one culture in particular, but are to reflect many in an ever-changing fictional fantasy world. Any inaccuracies and misrepresentations are not purposeful. If offense is taken by any individual or group of people, its doing was unintentional by the author.

The Six Races in the Zalian Chronicles do not represent any specific people groups or ethnicities. Each Race is a mixture of cultures, beliefs, and ethnicities. Excluding the Humans, the Races are to be seen as different species of God's highest creation, that being man-kind (symbolized more by the body, soul, and spirit aspect of humanity than anatomical similarities). These other Races (Dragon, Iaihagarian, Clapian/Thraknor, Gewban, and Kician) were created for imaginative and entertainment purposes and should not be regarded as anything more.

4

TABLE OF CONTENTS

BEFORE THE VERY FIRST LIGHT OF ANCIENT HISTORY,
THE MOST HIGH AND GOOD GOD EXISTED ALONE.
HE IS COMMONLY KNOWN AS
THE SHEPHERD,
THE SOWER,
OR
THE SHANKARICH
BUT HIS TRUE AND OLDEST NAME IS
AEIC.

BY HIS POWER AND HIS WISDOM,
THE WORLD OF ZALIA
WAS BROUGHT FORTH AND INHABITED BY THE SIX RACES:

THE IAIHAGARIANS,
CAVE-DWELLERS OF GREAT KNOWLEDGE AND SPIRITUALITY.
LOVERS OF PEACE AND THE WRITTEN WORD.

THE DRAGONS,
SKY-DWELLERS OF CUNNING AND FREEDOM.
LOVERS OF THE DANCE AND RIDDLES.

THE CLAPIANS,
ARCTIC-DWELLERS OF POWER AND FEROCITY.
LOVERS OF SONG AND MASONRY.

THE GEWBANS,
HILL-DWELLERS OF SERENITY AND EASE.
LOVERS OF NATURE AND NOURISHMENT.

THE KICIANS,
FOREST-DWELLERS OF BEAUTY AND SWIFTNESS.
LOVERS OF ART AND THE HUNT.

AND THE HUMANS.
LAND-DWELLERS OF INNOVATION AND TENACITY.
LOVERS OF OLD TRADITIONS AND NEW ADVANCEMENTS.

IN THAT DAY, ZALIA WAS GOOD.
BORN IN INNOCENCE AND PURITY.
FASHIONED IN RIGHTEOUSNESS

BUT THE TEMPTER, DRUL, CAME
AND DECEIVED THE SIX RACES OF THE WORLD.
THROUGH GUILE AND SUBTLETY, HE TURNED THEM
AGAINST THE ONE THAT HAD MADE THEM.

THAT WHICH WAS MADE TO BE GOOD WAS NOW
OVERCOME WITH EVIL.
AND A GREAT AND TERRIBLE WICKEDNESS
CONSUMED ALL LANDS

ALL SUFFERED AND TRAVAILED IN THEIR SIN.
TWISTING AND CONTORTING
IN CONFUSION AND SAVAGERY
AND IF LEFT TO THEMSELVES,
ALL WOULD WITHER TOWARDS DEATH AND DESTRUCTION
FOR ALL ETERNITY.

BUT AEIC,
WHOSE MERCY AND GRACE ARE INFINITE,
LOOKED DOWN UPON HIS FALLEN CREATION AND SAW THE
BONDAGE OF WICKEDNESS THAT THE WORLD WAS
DROWNING IN.
AND RATHER THAN JUSTLY TURNING TO
WRATH AND JUDGMENT,
HE WAS OVERWHELMED WITH
PITY AND COMPASSION.
HE WANTED TO BRING THEM BACK
TO HIS LOVING SIDE.

SO, IN ORDER TO GUIDE ALL PEOPLES OF THE WORLD
TOWARD THE LIGHT,
AEIC VOWED TO SEND HIS SON, IJEYOS, TO ZALIA.
IN THE YEAR OF 7602, IJEYOS WAS BORN OF A VIRGIN.
IJEYOS LIVED A PERFECT LIFE AND GAVE HIMSELF AS A
SACRIFICE FOR THE REDEMPTION OF ALL WHO WOULD CALL
UPON HIM IN REPENTANCE.

LONG BEFORE THAT DAY ARRIVED, AEIC CHOSE OUT MEN
AND WOMEN WHO HE SAW AS WORTHY. IN EACH LAND,
AEIC BESTOWED POWER UNTO HIS CHOSEN TO PROTECT
THEIR LAND FROM DARKNESS AND TO UPHOLD HIS LAWS.

IN THE EASTERN LAND OF DEDONAARC, AEIC BESTOWED
POWER ONTO A MAN CALLED VARK.
UPON THIS MAN, AEIC GAVE POWER OVER THE ELEMENTS.
A MASTER OF FIRE, WATER, WIND, EARTH, ICE, AND
LIGHTNING.

THROUGH VARK'S LINEAGE, MORE PROTECTORS WITH
SIMILAR ABILITIES WOULD COME.
THEY ARE THE VARKOAN.
THE FIVE VARKOAN.
THE FIVE CHOSEN DESCENDANTS OF VARK,

THE VARKOAN HAD EXTRAORDINARY POWER
TO EITHER BRING
PEACE AND SECURITY
OR
WAR AND CALAMITY.

AS EACH VARKOAN WOULD PASS ON,

A NEW VARKOAN WOULD BE CHOSEN.

IN THE EARLY SUMMER OF THE YEAR OF 7926, THERE STOOD NINE GREAT NATIONS:

MIRRAC, A WOODED NATION OF KNOWLEDGE AND POWER.

FERANDAR, A FOREST NATION OF CHARITY AND PROSPERITY.

CHEQWA, A DESERT NATION OF THE FIERCE AND MIGHTY.

ORIDION, A HILLED NATION OF BEAUTY AND AGRICULTURE.

HERTUE, A PLAINS NATION OF YOUTH AND TRADITION.

GRONK, A JUNGLE NATION OF ANCIENT RUINS AND RICH CULTURE.

CLAPIA, A FORSAKEN NATION OF MOUNTAINS AND SNOW.

SENTARAC, AN ISLAND NATION FILLED WITH THE BANISHED AND SCORNED.

AND THE SACRED NATION OF IJEYOS, BELOW IN THE UNDERGROUND TERRITORIES.

THIS TALE IS OF THE BEGINNING OF THE GREAT WAR OF THE NATIONS…

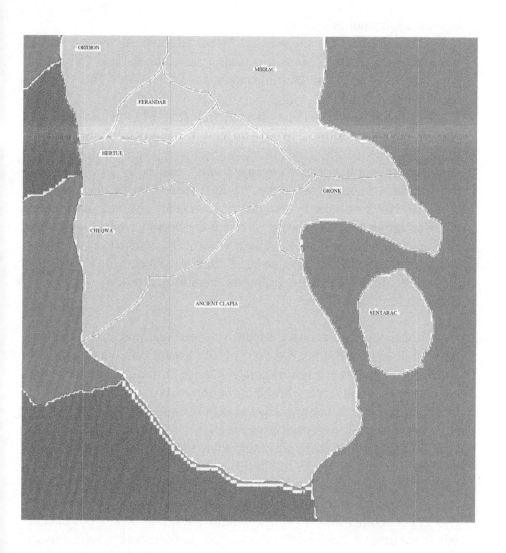

ORIDION

MIRRAC

FERANDAR

HERTUE

GRONK

CHEQWA

ANCIENT CLAPIA

SENTARAC

CHAPTER ONE
THE 'NOT-GOOD-THIEF'

My mother always said that border-crossing was a headache. Especially in troubling times.

I never knew how right she was until I started traveling. People would ask so many questions. Many unnecessary questions. Like "What is your business here?" or "Have any weapons on you?" or "Why are you dressed like a thief?"

Things would usually get complicated after that. My business was often nefarious and I tried to have at least one weapon on me at all times.

And I'm dressed like a thief because I *am* a thief.

So, one day I decided to skip the checks. I was in Mirrac, heading into Ferandar. Not so simple to do when there was a war going on between the two Nations. Soldiers were posted at the border, closely inspecting all who crossed in or out. Whether it was refugee, merchant, or noble, everyone was nearly stripped to see if they truly were who they said they were and if they had anything on them they shouldn't.

Couldn't have that for me.

It was long after sunset. Much was quiet and inactive. A good time for at least one soldier to doze off. At least, that's what I had hoped for. Sometimes I got fortunate enough to spot a soldier asleep at his post and I could creep right by him unnoticed.

I was not so lucky this time. The soldiers were awake. Maybe tired, but still very awake. That's what happens in times of war, I suppose. And, also unlucky for me, there was more than one patrol guarding the borders. There were three. In order to get out of one Nation and into another, people would have to be inspected by one group of soldiers, then, a dozen yards down the path, checked again. After the second check, yet another dozen yards down the path, they would be checked one more time. It was an efficient way to find something someone shouldn't have or spot someone who shouldn't be leaving/entering the Nation.

But I needed to be in Ferandar. In fact, I needed to be halfway across Ferandar before the next week. It was very important.

I needed a plan to get through the checks. I needed something that would keep the soldiers from looking too closely at me. However, at that disgustingly early hour, not many bright ideas were coming to mind.

That's when I spotted a Mirracian family. A mother and her two daughters.

Curious.

I didn't have any plans that would get me across, so I stayed put and watched them. The mother was about thirty years old, her daughters both looking below the age of seven. The only pack they had was slung around the mother's shoulder. Not exactly the most common group of travelers. They had no one with them to guard them. Plus, the mother didn't seem overly able to protect even herself, let alone her daughters. They didn't even have a weapon, from what I could tell. No supplies. No protection.

"A desperate family." I concluded. *"Running from something or someone for some reason."*

They were moving quickly but quietly down the path until the mother spotted the first checkpoint.

Then, she halted dead in her tracks.

Minutes passed. Many minutes passed. The mother didn't move. On her face, I clearly examined concern, worry, and possibly even panic under a guise of control. She was continually staring at the soldiers down the road with a shudder in her breathing as she clung to her two daughters' hands tightly.

I grinned under my mask. Not only had my suspicions been confirmed, but other questions had been answered as well. This was a good opportunity for me.

"Need to get across?" I spoke to them.

The family was startled. They hadn't seen me sitting there.

For long moments, they were all frozen, staring at me with a dreadful fear.

I tended to have that affect.

But, upon removing my hood and mask, they began to calm.

"It's okay." I promised with a smile. "We're in the same boat. I need to get across, too. Perhaps we can help each other?"

"How?" The mother questioned me in a crisp, Mirracian accent.

"Well, you seem like you don't want to be stopped by those soldiers ahead." I mentioned. "Whether you're hiding an item or your identity, it doesn't matter to me. The fact is, you need someone at your side to ensure those soldiers don't give you a closer look."

The woman never answered, but I could tell by her face that I wasn't wrong.

"And, I need the very same thing." I continued.

"That still doesn't answer my question." The mother scowled, still suspicious. "How can you get us across without the soldiers stopping us?"

"Can you act?" I asked.

"What does that have to do with anything?" The woman twisted her lips uncomfortably.

"The key is a uniform." I told her. "And acting like you know what you're doing. If you have those things, people will rarely question you."

"But neither of us have a uniform." The woman pointed out.

"Yet." I replied.

A bathroom break. It's the perfect time to jump someone. First off, there was the distracting, trickling noise to keep the soldier from hearing me close by. Secondly, his guard was down. Thirdly, even if he was still wary of his surroundings, what could he do if he noticed I was there? He'd have to yank up his pants before he could reach for his sword.

All in all, it was an easy take down. The soldier started peeing. I slammed his head into the tree. No one even heard him yelp. By the time he would wake up, both me and his armor would be far away.

I approached the family, now wearing the soldiers uniform and armor.

"They won't just let us through because you look like a soldier." The mother worried. "And they'll know one of their comrades is missing. This won't work!"

"It will." I reassured her.

"And if it doesn't?"

"If it doesn't…" I sighed, patting the stolen sword on my belt. "I know how to use this."

The mother seemed only further frightened by that comment. She looked to her young daughters, obviously concerned for their safety.

"But-" She began to argue.

"You will reach the other side." I interrupted her. "All of you will. You just have to trust me."

"That's asking a lot." The woman glared. "I don't even know you."

I couldn't deny that.

"Well, then do you want to try going through without me?" I offered, gesturing down the path.

The mother considered it for a moment, her eyes flicking between me and the road.

"…No."

"Halt." A soldier ordered sleepily at the first check. About six other soldiers stood around him, also looking very weary. Other soldiers were about, patrolling the border, but only six stood on the path.

We stopped. I snapped to attention in the way I had seen Mirracian soldiers do before.

"No need for that." The soldier responded lazily. "Who are you and why are you going into Ferandar?"

"Name's Benjamin. I'm heading to the front, sir." I stated simply, returning to a casual stance.

"What about them?" The soldier pointed to the woman with her daughters.

"My mother and sisters, sir." I replied. "They want to see me off."

The soldier looked at all of us with tired eyes. "Whatever. Go on through."

The next check was a tad more difficult. Same amount of soldiers guarding the road, but much more awake. Thankfully, they seemed to be in a good mood. They were joking amongst themselves when we neared them. The soldier in charge simply held his hand up in a "stop" motion. He didn't say anything because he was laughing at whatever one of his comrades had just said.

I snapped to attention as before. This time it was noted and appreciated.

"At ease." The soldier finally recovered from laughing. "Business in Ferandar?"

"I'm off to fight against the Ferandarons after last month's great loss, sir."

15

That sobered up the soldiers fairly quickly. A month ago, the Mirracians had lost hundreds of men in a terrible ambush from the Ferandaron army.

The soldier cleared his throat uncomfortably. "You're one of the new recruits?"

"No, sir." I responded. "Returning."

"Returning?" The soldiers scratched his chin.

"Badly wounded." I explained. "I was sent back home to recover. I've healed and I want to get back out there."

"Why so eager?"

"My father died in that battle." I told him.

The soldier's jaw hung loose. "Oh...I'm...I'm very sorry, son."

"Thank you, sir."

"These your family?" He pointed to the others with me.

I nodded. "I promised them I'd take them to where he's buried."

The soldier sighed heavily, buying my story. He said nothing else, but just gestured for us to pass through.

One more to go.

Unfortunately, this last one was unlike either checks. No soldier was tired, but no soldier was joking around, either. All were serious, standing straight, ready for action. Twelve of them stood on the path. In the middle of the twelve was an elder, but strong, stern officer. His face was as hard as stone. His eyes were unwavering, spearing at me like daggers.

I was feeling nervous. He was examining everything about me as I walked towards him.

I swallowed and snapped to attention as we came close enough.

"Well, this isn't suspicious in the least." The man snarled with curled lips. "Just a young Mirracian soldier with his family, strolling into Ferandar in the dead of night."

The officer snapped his fierce eyes at the soldiers around him. "Search their belongings for anything out of place."

The mother and I surrendered our packs for inspection. Thankfully, I didn't have anything condemning in my pack. In fact, I didn't really have anything at all in my pack. Just a sketching and some berries I had picked earlier that day. The mother only had food in her pack. Needless to say, we were given back our packs without much questioning.

But the officer wasn't done with us.

"Explain yourselves." He snooted.

I took a deep breath before answering. "We've traveled far, sir. I wish to return to my company."

"Where?"

"Verechel." I said quickly. "Where the great lo-"

"Why bring them?" The officer peered at the mother and daughters behind me. "Who are they to you?

"My mother and little sisters. They are going to see me off." I explained. "It is customary to do so, isn't it?"

"Only if you're a fool." The officer sneered. "If you were truly a soldier of Mirrac, you would have left them behind."

"...Sir?"

"You are lying." The man pointed with an accusing finger. "First, the company at Verechel was disbanded into the companies at Bithicar and Sutton. The reason for this was because there were hardly any men left in that company after last month's slaughter. You would have been given orders notifying you of this and would have been sorted accordingly. Secondly, a man who had been a part of said company would have known better than to drag his family along with him into enemy territory directly after being *ambushed*. Thirdly, they are *not* your family. This woman is not even ten years your senior, yet you claim to be her son. Fourthly, this armor you are wearing...it's not yours. The breastplate is too big for you. You stole this armor, I assume. Your story is, at best, fraudulent. You are hiding something, therefore, you shall be detained until we can discover who you truly are."

With that, the officer motioned for his men to take us. I felt the woman behind me shiver in fear. In her mind, we were caught.

But I knew how to deal with pompous, authoritative pea-brains.

"If I may, sir." I said gently. "I can explain all of that."

The soldiers hesitated, glancing back at their commanding officer.

"Can you now?" The officer chuckled. "Do try. It'll humor me."

"In that ambush, I was terribly wounded." I began. "I was struck down by a Ferandaron axeman who also wounded my father. The axeman cut through my breastplate and sliced part of my chest open. I was not expected to survive, but was rushed to a healer and saved. My father was not so lucky. Because my breastplate was damaged, I took my father's. Partly out of need. Partly out of desire to keep it in honor of his memory. Immediately after, I was brought home in Mirrac to my family where I could recover. I healed remarkably well and quickly left to return to the war to avenge my father's death. So quickly, in fact, that I didn't even report to any other Mirracian officers or soldiers. I have not been updated on the war until now, sir. For that, I thank you. As for my mother, she is thirty-two years old. I am sixteen. She had me when she was sixteen herself. After all, young marriages are extremely common in Mirrac. And finally, concerning the fact that I am willing to bring my family into enemy territory. My mother here is now a widow. My sisters, fatherless. They begged me, *pleaded* with me, that I would show them the place of our father's burial. Can you blame them for endangering themselves so that they can pay their respects to a man they loved so much?"

The officer took this all in. His soldiers glanced at him, awaiting his orders.

"Even if that pathetic story was true, you can't prove any of that." The officer huffed.

It was hard not to give a smug smirk at that moment.

"Can't I?" I asked, removing my breastplate. I laid it on the ground and pulled open my Mirracian shirt.

From my left shoulder all the way down to the right side of my waist was a long, gaping scar.

A scar from a battle axe.

The officer's eyes widened in surprise.

His soldiers looked at each other, satisfied that I had just proven my story.

Before long, the mother, her daughters, and I were all in Ferandar.

"You have saved me and my daughters." The woman told me as she laid her children to bed. We were some distance away from the border of Mirrac and Ferandar. We were safe. I had made a fire and was now stoking it.

"I never should have doubted you." The woman continued. "How can I repay you?"

"No need." I smiled at her, grateful to be in my regular clothes again. "I picked several of those soldier's pockets. That officer had an especially good amount of coin in his wallet."

18

I pulled out the wallet and tossed it to the woman
She gazed inside it and gasped at how full it was.
"Why are you giving this to me?" She spoke breathlessly.
"I don't know why you wanted to flee Mirrac." I admitted. "But if
you're going to start a new life elsewhere, you'll need money."
"But what about you?" She asked.
"Don't worry." I smiled. "I stole enough for me."
The woman sat down next to me without saying anything for a while.
A look was in her eyes. It was somewhere between relief and
thoughtfulness.
"My name is Rachel." She said to me. "And I am running away from
my husband."
I said nothing in response. Honestly, I didn't really want to exchange
personal stories or reasons, but she seemed like she needed to get it off
her chest.
"My husband is a well-known authority in Mirrac." Rachel continued.
"He answers to the king himself, though he's never told me what he is
exactly. He's abusive and a very angry man. Especially when he
doesn't get his way."
Hints of tears were moistening her eyes. "He's hurt me before. He's
hurt my daughters. Too often, he's hurt us. I...I just can't let my
daughters live there anymore."
"And you were afraid the soldiers at the border would recognize you."
I concluded. I gestured towards her fiery-red hair. It wasn't a very
common hair color in Mirrac.
She nodded, touching her hair. "It was a gamble."
"What do you plan to do?" I asked her.
"Well, in Ferandar, I can disappear." Rachel shrugged. "Sounded better
than my current situation."
"Don't stay in Ferandar." I told her.
"Don't?" She raised her eyebrows.
"With the war that's going on, who knows what the outcome will be?"
I said. "Mirrac's already winning against Ferandar. And I don't know if
they'll stop there. Go as far as Oridion. There's a massive mixture of
people there, so you can blend in even as a foreigner. Also, if Mirrac's
war goes that far, you can flee into the Nation of Malnovey."
Rachel thought on this, beginning to nod at my advice. "Okay."

"Do you have a trade that you can live off of and provide for your daughters?" I quizzed her.

"...No."

"Then, once you get in Oridion, head to the city of Bardenwei." I instructed. "There are several wealthy households there that take in servants all the time. If you can, find the Leopold household. I've seen how he treats people and he's very kind."

"Leopold." Rachel repeated. "Thank you so much. Thank you again."

"No problem." I turned to the stolen Mirracian gear. I picked up the Mirracian sword. "You'll need this. There are plenty of unpleasant people in both Ferandar and Oridion. That number will increase if they find out you're Mirracian. You should try and hide your accent as best as you can."

Rachel hesitantly took the sword. "But what about you?"

"I can take care of myself." I assured her. "I don't need a sword right now."

"But where are you going?"

"I'll be where I need to be." I replied. "I just need to be halfway through Ferandar by next week."

"Why?"

I shuffled uncomfortably. I wasn't about to start confessing my secrets to a stranger.

"I just need to be there."

Rachel took the hint. She changed subjects. "I'm only twenty-five, just so you know."

I groaned. "Sorry."

"It's fine, truly." Rachel smiled genuinely. "I get it all the time. People always tell me I looked older than I really am."

"It was a good age to use if you were going to be my mother." I told her.

Rachel didn't respond to that for a while. She just kept looking at me. Then, she spoke again. "You are Ferandaron."

"Of a sort." I shrugged.

"What were you doing in Mirrac?" Rachel asked.

"...Looking for someone." I said vaguely, thinking about the sketch in my pack. "A man I used to know."

"Hm." Rachel grunted. "And you are a thief, right?"

I was rather surprised by that question. "Um, yes I am."

Rachel shrugged. "You don't seem like one. You could have robbed me and my daughters when you first found us. But you helped us. You gave me advice. You gave me money. You gave me a sword. You've, essentially, rescued me and my daughters. I've just never heard of a thief that would do any of those things."

"Don't let me fool you." I shook my head. "I rob people all the time. I robbed four soldiers tonight. I only helped you because you would help me. Plus, you and your daughters had nothing worthy of stealing and I'm not that vicious of a bandit."

Rachel smiled genuinely. "Whatever you say."

I got the feeling she wasn't believing a word I had said. I sighed and turned away from her.

"Well, does the 'not-good-thief' have a name?" Rachel asked me, still smiling. "Or is it really 'Benjamin'?"

"No. It's Nathan." I muttered.

"Then, Nathan, I pray that the Shepherd blesses you for your selfless deed. And may fortune and goodness find you."

I narrowed my eyes as I stared into the fire. "I don't intend for fortune to find me. I expect to find it."

We didn't talk anymore that night. Rachel joined her daughters in sleep as I sat next to the fire, watching the stars.

Even if I had wanted to go to sleep, I would have had trouble doing it that night.

I had a lot on my mind.

Mostly, a tune. A poem that was read to me long ago.

When the leaves bud forth
And warmth fills the days
It is a sign to come home again
When winter's chill ends
With the sunlight's rays
It is a sign to come home again

Home in the fields of growing corn
Home in the houses hid in misty morns

Home is where you will head, my son

21

Home in my arms is where you belong

I sighed, still watching the stars. "Home…"

CHAPTER TWO
A VERY SPECIAL BIRTHDAY

I pulled up my mask as I spied a trio of servants hanging out their master's laundry.

I was in Thusheree, a fishing village. Nearly all of the houses there were structured directly next to the river. However, to my advantage, the town left much of the trees and foliage alone. That gave me many places to hide in.

I needed some items. I only had a short amount of time to get those items and head out. A very special occasion was arriving in three days and I needed to be in a place known as Garlíetno. It was very important to me and for it, I wanted to look nice for once. If I was going to get something nice to wear, it was going to come from the wealthiest man in Thusheree: Hector.

I had robbed Hector before, though it had been a terrible idea. The man was a retired war general that wanted to live the rest of his days sitting by the river and getting as fat as he possibly could. But the man was a brute. He was hated by almost everyone he knew, though they would never tell him that. He had a fierce temper, an entitlement mentality, and an attitude so nasty that he could wilt flowers with it.

That being said, it was so enjoyable to rob from him. But it was also very dangerous. This man had been through his share of war and he had plenty of servants that knew how to fight with multiple weapons. The last time I stole from Hector, I nearly lost both of my hands. But that was only because I had been seen.

This time, I would be invisible.

Hector's house was built like a mansion. The man had no family living with him (which never surprised me) but had dozens of rooms. Each room was devoted to a different purpose: entertainment, feasting, talking with guests, admiring art, or even just lounging around. He had it all. His staff of servants and guards were all given just one, tiny, bare room to sleep in. Though they worked for him, they had no love for their master. Why would they? He treated them like dirt.

But that didn't mean he didn't pay them well. He had more money than he knew what to do with. And because of how well paid his servants were, they learned how to put up with him. In fact, they not only tolerated him, but did everything he commanded quickly and efficiently.

And, if I was caught, it very possibly would mean my life would end. But life isn't fun if you don't take risks. Off I went.

I ran up towards Hector's house, making sure I was out of the line of sight of the servants who were hanging laundry. In situations like this, it was best to have a plan, but I was no good at making any. I usually just improvised. So far, improvisation never steered me wrong. I was still alive and had all my appendages, fingers, and even toes.

What could go wrong?

I reached a side door and slipped in silently. I was welcomed by a bright, breezy room that was filled with plant-life. Flowers, small trees, and exotic plants were everywhere. I glanced up to see panels near the ceiling that were opened to allow sunlight to come through. I grinned under my mask. Flowers just happened to be one of the things I needed. But I wasn't going to steal any yet. I wanted to keep the flowers alive as long as possible. This was the last thing I would snatch before leaving. I snuck through the room, noting which flowers I might take.

I came to a door that led further into the house and eased it open ever so slightly.

Noise of servants working came immediately. I took an uncomfortable breath. I admit that I was arrogant. I was stealing in the middle of the day from someone who had plenty of people watching over his stuff. However, I wasn't so proud that I didn't get nervous at the sound of people busy-ing through a house I was robbing.

I closed the door and took a moment to actually think.

Trying to stay invisible in a circumstance like this wasn't going to work. Any corner could have another armed servant waiting behind it. No, sneaking wouldn't work.

Blending in would.

It wasn't hard to snatch a servant uniform. There were plenty hanging outside, drying. I even found one my size. It fit perfectly, albeit damp.

I hustled through the house, not even being noticed by most servants. There was so much work to be done that it was so easy to just hurry past busy servants. The swords on their belts made me uncomfortable, but something else weighed heavier on my mind: I was rather lost. The house was so huge, it was taking me much longer than I thought it would to find anything. And, if I kept looking around like I didn't know where anything was, someone was bound to start noticing and ask questions.

Questions that I probably wouldn't be able to answer.

And then the swords on their belts would be much more of a problem.

So, after searching through five different rooms, I gave up and asked a nearby servant girl.

"Excuse me." I tapped her on the shoulder while she was kneading bread.

She turned and gave a quizzical look at me. "Who are you?"

"Benjamin." I responded quickly. "I'm new."

"New?" She furrowed her brow. "Elias didn't say we were getting any new helpers."

"Well, Master Hector did." I shrugged. "Says he's been disappointed in some of his staff, lately. Actually, I think he did say something about a guy named Elias who wasn't earning his keep."

A look of fear sprouted on her face. "He's going to fire Elias? He's worked here for nearly ten years!"

"Hey, everyone's expendable." I replied. "Guy better shape up or he's a goner. Now, can you help me?"

The servant girl put down her dough and turned to me. "Uh, sure."

"Where is the room where Master Hector keeps all of his nice clothes?"

The servant girl looked at me suspiciously. "Shouldn't you know that? Were you not told anything when Master Hector hired you?"

I swallowed, feeling my forehead bead with sweat. I tried to think of a quick answer.

"Master Hector said he didn't want to take the time to tell me everything." I spat out. "Said he was tired and that I'd need to figure it out myself."

The servant girl rolled her eyes. "That sounds like him."

She pointed down a hallway. "Fifth door on the right."

"Thanks!"

It took me a while to find a suit I liked. None of them were my size, but one of his older suits was close enough. It was a gorgeous blue military uniform, hinted with yellow here and there. It smelled slightly moldy, but beggars can't be choosers. I slung it over my back as I headed for the door.

As I took hold of the handle, I made a mental note that I would need to be faster and more careful now. I was carrying around one of Hector's suits and that would be suspicious. Especially since it was a uniform that no longer fit Hector's massive bulk. Servants would be wondering why I had it.

"*Just two more items and then I'm gone.*" I thought to myself and went into the hallway.

I tried my best to seem inconspicuous. I was still able to pass most servants without them asking me any questions. Most would give me a puzzled look. All I had to do was say "Master wants to see his old uniforms. He's feeling reminiscent" and most of them would nod and leave me be.

There was one, however, that did stop me.

"What are you doing with that?" He pointed to the uniform.

"Master wants to see his old uniforms. He's feeling reminiscent." I repeated, hoping he would let me go.

The servant scratched his chin. "That's strange. He just told Elias he was going to take a nap."

"Ohhh." I said, shaking my head sadly.

"'Ohhh'?" The servant asked.

I motioned for him to come closer. He leaned in a bit.

"Master isn't happy with Elias." I whispered to him. "When he hired me, he told me that Elias has been nothing but a thorn in his side recently. He doesn't trust him at all, for some reason. I think he's going to throw him out."

"No!" The servant gasped. "Elias? But he's been here for years! He's done nothing wrong! Why would Master Hector fire him?"

I shrugged. "You know the master. He's irrational. Get him in a bad mood and he'll throw **anybody** in the fire."

Then I motioned for him to come even closer. The servant got close enough for me to whisper to him.

"That means us too. We need to watch each other's backs. Two are better than one, right?"

"Right. Right." The servant nodded.

"Speaking of which, I need your help." I told him. "Master Hector also wanted some candles and I can't seem to remember where he keeps them. Help out a friend?"

"Of course, buddy." The servant smiled. "On the south wing. They're in the same room as the Cheqwan skins and rugs."

"Thank you so much."

I bagged seven candles after checking through Hector's collection. I was snickering to myself as I exited the room. All I needed now was to go back to the garden room, take some flowers that I liked, and I'd be on my merry way.

"I don't know why I was worrying so much." I thought. *"This was so easy."*

Suddenly, a tall, older man was approaching me in the hallway. He gave a long, cold stare at me and Hector's uniform.

"What do you think you're doing with that?" He stopped me in the hallway.

"Just getting it to the master." I informed him. "He wants to take a trip down memory lane. Look at his old uniforms and such."

"The master didn't tell me." The servant raised an eyebrow.

"Why should he?" I asked him, getting slightly nervous at his penetrating stare. "Every servant is busy, after all. And since Elias has been in trouble with him, Master Hector is probably looking for someone else to be his loyal attendant."

"Elias is in trouble, huh?" The man questioned.

"Yeah, it's so sad." I nodded. "The master hired me, telling me all about it. I think he wants to replace him. Who knows? I might take his place."

The man curled his lip as he bent lower to look me right in the eye. *"I'm* Elias."

A moment of petrifying silence passed.

"And, the master *never* hires servants." Elias continued. "He has *me* do that because he's too lazy."

Another terrifying moment of silence.

Elias put his hand on his sword. "Now, tell me who you are and what you're doing here, or-"

I kicked Elias between the legs, making him wheeze and drop to the floor.

From there, I was sprinting. Running as fast as my legs could carry me.

"Thief! Thief! Stop him!" Elias pointed, crying in a high voice.

Every servant in my path instantly pulled out swords.

Not good. I took a second to pray.

Then, I charged head-on at them. Thieving was my craft, my trade.

And, from what I've come to learn, you need to be fast in order to steal *and* live.

Thankfully, I was fast.

I raced through each servant, barely missing the edge of a blade more times then I'd like to admit.

I burst through the garden room door, several servants chasing after me. I ripped three random flowers out of the closest pot and kicked the outside door open.

From there, I was safe. The servants could chase me, but they would ultimately lose me.

Nature was my home and I knew it better than anyone. Before they could run into the bushes, I was undetectable to them.

They tried to find me, but it was no good. All they found was the servant uniform I was wearing.

And as I was sneaking away, I heard a deafening roar come from Hector's house:

"A thief got away with *what*?!"

It was most definitely Hector.

"ELIAS!!!"

"Job security is so hard to come by these days." I laughed to myself.

The suit was terribly uncomfortable, but I ignored it as best as I could. I held the flowers in my hands and the candles were in my pack.

I had finally made it to Garlíetno.

It was my home village. The place of my birth.

It had once been a large, thriving village that lied twenty miles west of the capitol city, Iarrag.

But now?

Abandoned.

Desolate.

Empty.

The only remnant of life that remained there were animals. They made their homes in the decaying, destroyed buildings that had once been a part of my village. All that I used to know lay in ruin. Much of it was covered in vines and nettles now.
The sight brought sorrow to my heart and tears to my eyes.
But it was no time to cry. I was here for a reason.
At the center of the village a broken down monument. It used to be a large pillar that had the law of the Shepherd written on it.
I set down the flowers before the base of the destroyed monument and began taking out the candles. I lit the candles and placed them around the flowers. I took a moment to bow and pray to the Shepherd.
However, my prayer was more out of tradition than from my heart.
It's hard to be thankful when you have nothing.
I rose up from bowing and took out my flute. I gazed at it for several minutes, just remembering. It was the last thing I had from my parents. Before I put it to my lips and began filling the air with its soothing whispers, I softly uttered three words:
"Happy birthday, Father."

CHAPTER THREE
UNEXPECTED ENCOUNTERS

The sun began to rise. I was waking up right as the shining sunlight crept in through the broken windows. The morning light brought warmth to my chilled body. I took a deep breath and sighed slowly. After some quick stretching, I rose and gazed out of the windows. I took in the beauty of the sunrise as it peeked over the hills. I always loved the colors the sun brought when it first showed itself. Had I some paint and something to paint on, I would try to capture its magnificence.

Key word being "try". I was a terrible painter.

I sat there for a while, just watching the beautiful oranges and golds as the blazing orb of fire rose from the horizon.

But I didn't have time to waste. It was time to get to work.

It was the morning after my father's birthday. I had traveled through the night to where I was living now: essentially nowhere.

All I had to stay in was a broken down shack that had been abandoned in the density of the woods. Me and my friend Korhn lived there, far away from where travelers often strode.

It wasn't healthy for a thief if everyone knew where he lived.

My robbing spot was a couple miles from where Korhn and I lived. A popular rode to Iarrag. It worked rather well that way. Every now and again, I would get an unsuspecting traveler coming down my way and I'd relieve him of some…unnecessary riches. Most of the time, they never even missed what I stole. But that was because I stole from those who had more than enough. People who's pockets were heavy.

Beggars? Widows? Peasants?

No.

Stealing from those who already had so little…I couldn't find it in myself to do it. Besides, it's not like I would get anything good from them.

Arriving at my robbing spot a couple of hours later, I began setting up for a good stealing. After getting prepared, I waited. I was hidden up in a sturdy oak tree that looked over most of the road. It was early morning, so I didn't expect too many people coming down the road. Even if they did, I would need Korhn before I could really do anything. Then, as if he heard my thoughts, I was startled by the sound of chittering behind me. Turning about, I found that Korhn had snuck up behind me. Korhn was my pet raccoon. If you could call him a pet. Most of the time, he acted like he was the one in charge. He had almost convinced me to take him along when I ventured to Mirrac, but I decided against it.

He chattered as he nibbled on a small nut. I snatched it away from him. "Don't eat that." I whispered.

He glanced up at me, his eyes begging me behind his natural mask. "Don't look at me like that. Raccoons don't eat acorns."

But we were both interrupted by the sound of horse hooves moving across the road. I watched earnestly down the road from the shadows of my tall tree. I hoped that it would be our breakfast. As the sound of the hooves came closer, I noticed that the horses were pulling a carriage. I inspected the carriage for signs of wealth. The curtains that draped over the windows were made of fine velvet and the beautiful woodwork of the coach was magnificent.

I grinned to Korhn. "Expensive, wouldn't you say?"

The one riding in the marvelous carriage was no beggar. Judging by the look and size of the carriage, it had been on a long journey. The state of the driver also confirmed that. His eyes were drooping frequently, his shoulders were slumped over, and he was yawning every few minutes.

People usually brought food on long journeys.

"And you wanted to eat an acorn." I nudged Korhn. "Not today. We're gonna get some *real* food."

With that, Korhn snickered and started hopping.

"Okay, okay. Don't get too excited." I peered out onto the road. The carriage was getting closer.

"All right, go cut the line." I whispered to Korhn. He scampered off quickly as the carriage was almost right underneath me.

Nearly a minute later, a loud creaking sound echoed out. The driver began pulling violently on the reigns as a tall, dead tree collapsed onto the road. The tree covered the entire path. There was no getting around it.

"Well, that's lovely." The driver groaned sarcastically.

I snickered as I pulled my mask up just below my eyes. I had been waiting for a while to pull that trick. It had taken me a great deal of time and effort to saw through the trunk of the tree. Once I had chipped through the trunk, I tied some old, stolen rope to a low branch. I took the rest of the rope and attached it to another strong tree so it would hold it up.

In order to fall, the line simply needed to be cut.

Which Korhn did perfectly.

I immediately got to work. I slipped silently down on top of the carriage and waited until the rider left his seat inside. He had left his door ajar.

"What happened, Lewis?" I heard the rider ask as I slinked down the back of the carriage. With my pick, I silently unlatched the lock and opened the back doors. The back of the carriage had a couple sacks full of food. Salted meats, dried fruits, and such like. I quickly began to take as much food as I could out of the sacks. Snickering as I bagged my prize, I thought I was home free with more food than I had seen in months, until…

Until I heard that one sound that ruined my chances…

A very tiny, simple sound…

A gasp.

A small, scared-sounding gasp. My eyes widened at the sound and I immediately looked up. Sitting in the second seat of the carriage, peeking over the seat at me, was none other than a princess. There was no mistake. She was dressed in a beautiful white dress that was arrayed with pearls and diamonds. On her head, she wore a small but very stunning tiara. She had long brown hair and bright, lovely blue eyes. And I thought the sunrise was beautiful. She was radiant.

For a moment, we both froze.

I knew who she was. I had seen her before, parading through major cities.

She was Princess Sophia. The firstborn and only daughter of King William and Queen Terra of Ferandar.

"Princess Sophia?" I whispered nearly silently. But the girl was too frightened to answer.

My thoughts raced. *"That means…this carriage…is the **king's**?!"*

"*Ceruxda!*" I gasped.

Suddenly, the princess's voice returned.
"Father! Father! Come quickly!" She cried. I began to panic. I was flat-out terrified to think what would happen if King William found me **stealing** from his carriage and frightening his beloved child. He wasn't necessarily the forgiving type. He didn't like thieves either. He would have a gallows with my name on it. Knowing that, I tried to get out of there as quick as I could. So quickly, in fact, that I forgot I was halfway in the back of the carriage. I tried to get out, but hit my head in the process. This made me drop all of the food I had grabbed, but I ignored it. I scurried up to the top of the coach and leaped to a branch of my tree. I ran up it and immediately concealed myself. I became invisible to everything around me.
"What is it, Sophia?!" King William asked as my heart was still racing.
"There...There was a boy here."
"A boy?" William Questioned.
"Sire." The driver, Lewis, came running to the king. He had my rope in his hands. "Look."
William stared at it. "This tree was meant to fall. Bandits!"
"Yes! Yes!" Sophia agreed. "The boy was wearing the attire of a bandit! He wore a hooded dark-green cloak, with a dark-green mask and brown tunic and pants. He had these..." She paused as if she was in a trance. "...Soft silver eyes."
"Lewis, we need to get back to the castle." King William returned to his seat.
"Another road, then, Sire?" Lewis asked as he returned to the perch.
"Yes, and hurry." The king sounded rather anxious.
They turned the carriage around and sped away. Korhn came to my side and started chattering wildly.
"Yes, I know." I sighed. "She saw me, but don't worry. I have my mask on. I look identical to any other bandit around these parts."
I paused.
"Except my eyes...which she clearly noticed."
I grumbled as they rode off...
With our food.
My stomach growled miserably.
Korhn climbed up on my shoulder. He began to chitter again.

"Follow her?" I questioned harshly. "Oh, absolutely, yes. Follow her. That's a wonderful idea. Death is always such an honorable pursuit." But Korhn reasoned with me.

Ferandar, of course, was at war with Mirrac. A war can be a lovely distraction. The soldiers were all at the border, fighting, and most of the palace guards were protecting Ferandar's cities. King William was a king of the people, and he did not wish for them to suffer. He cared a good deal for his Nation and people. This meant that the king's castle was short on guards, which also meant the treasury of the kingdom was short on guards. I pondered over this.

"Not a good idea." I judged. "We've never tried to break into a treasury before. You got a plan for that?"

Korhn stared at me with a blank expression.

"I'll take that as a 'no'." I sighed.

My stomach rumbled again.

I groaned. "I don't like this idea...but we've gotten away with worse ones. Fine."

Korhn and I began heading towards Iarrag, King William's palace.

I hoped it would not be the last day I saw the sun rise.

The towers of the king's castle of Iarrag gleamed in the lowering sun. Built tough, but not at the expense of majesty. Numerous blue and yellow banners hung in places many would see as unnecessary, but who was I to judge? I sat on a hill, trying to figure out a way in. Iarrag was in a valley, surrounded by hills. It was very easy to scope out. The walls of Iarrag, though not as guarded as the walls to the palace, still had enough guards to intimidate. And why shouldn't there be? If I was king, I'd prefer to be protected. Although, King William was probably more concerned with his wife and child's protection than his own. Inside the walls was the large city that was intended for common-folk. Not lowly peasants, but certainly not royalty. Men and women with some stature and reputation, but not much more than that. Simple homes, bakeries, smiths, stables, mills, and other such places were seen all around the bustling city of Iarrag. Pleasant fountains and shrubbery were here and there. Rich farmlands lied on the outside of the city. I was able to snatch a few carrots from these farms. Korhn and I munched on them as we waited for the king and the princess to arrive. Because they had to turn around and take a different road, we made it to Iarrag long before they did. That was lucky, for the carriage was our ticket in. Fortunately, King William had not realized the back of the carriage had been unlatched. We were going to sneak in, only this time we wouldn't get caught…hopefully. The guards would open the gates immediately and without question. This was said much easier than done, though. While Korhn and I hid in the shade of some trees near the road, the coach arrived. I signaled Korhn. Korhn ran out of the brush and violently hissed at the horses. The horses were spooked by this sudden surprise. They began to whiny and buck. The driver was very much distracted. I pulled up my mask and bolted out from my hiding place. I jumped onto the back of the carriage and opened the back as gently as possible.

This was the most dangerous part of the plan. I had to move into the back of the carriage without being seen by King William or Princess Sophia. Looking back on it, this really was a stupid plan.

Regardless, I did it anyway. I was able to open the back without making any noise. But suddenly…

"What now?!" King William exclaimed. He began to shift around in the carriage. If he turned enough, he would see me. I began to panic again. If he saw me, I was dead. We were very close to the castle. The king could call dozens of guards that were just a shout's distance away. I couldn't afford that. In desperation, I dove into their trunk.

William didn't see me. Korhn soon joined me in the back under piles of clothing and such. The coach started to move again after the horses calmed down. As I wondered why they had so much luggage, I eavesdropped on the two royals.

"Must have been a snake that spooked the horses." William muttered.

"Father, I'm scared." Sophia whimpered.

"Of what, my dear?"

"That thief." She explained. "If it wasn't for me, he would have stolen all of the food. Do you think he'll want revenge?"

Korhn looked at me with a look of confusion.

"She makes me sound like Stephen." I thought.

"Now, now, Sophia. He won't ever reach us. Even if he does want revenge, he'll never get the chance."

I scoffed silently.

"Why," The king laughed. "He wouldn't even be able to sneak in this carriage again. Not with our keen, sharp eyes."

Irony.

"Open the gates!" A man yelled from at the top of the walls. I smiled as I let out a sigh of relief.

"Father, did you hear that?" The princess asked.

I widened my eyes. "...*There's no way she could have heard that.*"

"Hear what?"

"A deep breath..." Sophia kept her voice low. "I heard something. I know I did."

"*Ceruxda!*" I began getting very scared. I glared at Korhn, silently accusing him. "*This was **your** idea!*"

"Shh..." King William whispered. I felt something moving the sack on top of me. The king lifted it to see the very thief that robbed him before. His eyes grew as wide as cup saucers. I laughed nervously.

"Guards!" He screamed. In desperation, I threw my fist and struck him in the jaw. He instantly fell back in his seat, somewhat dazed. I reached for the back doors of the coach as Princess Sophia shrieked.

"It's the thief! Dear goodness! He's come back for me!"

I flipped myself up onto the top of the carriage as guards rushed over to arrest me.

"Halt, Bandit!" One exclaimed. I noticed I was already inside the city walls. I jumped from the coach and fled into the city. The guards followed after me, but no castle guard can catch a thief. They were accustomed to standing and watching most of the time. Running was *my* expertise. But I also had no idea where I was going. I had never been in Iarrag before. Fortunately, the city marketplace wasn't too far from the gates. Commoners were everywhere. Being the market, vast amounts of people were there and many of them were carrying large loads of items. I had two options: blend in with the crowd or knock people down to help detain the guards after me.

Considering what I was wearing, I chose the latter option. I shoved over dozens of people. A man carrying fresh meat, a woman carrying a basket of apples, a baker with a tray of bread, anyone I could that would put up obstacles for my pursuers. The plan was working as the guards were becoming more distant from me. However, I needed a place to hide. Once I was out of the guards' sight, I noticed a gutter.

A gutter.

It was disgusting.

It was rank.

But I could slink through it.

And it did save my life.

"We need to lie low for a couple of hours, maybe a day." I whispered to Korhn after the guards had lost my trail. I was peeking out the gutter drain from inside the sewers.

"This was a very bad idea." I groaned. "Why did I listen to you?"

Korhn nuzzled my arms.

I glanced down at him. "What?"

Korhn nodded down the sewer. I peered down there. There were branches of sewer lines leading here and there. I scratched my head. The sewers were spread throughout Iarrag. It was a newer thing to help keep the castle clean of...stuff. Stuff that I was knee deep in.

But they could lead outside the castle walls.

"We could possibly find our way out through these tunnels." I noted to Korhn.

Then I had a thought.

"Or...they could lead us in."

Korhn gazed up at me.

The sewers could lead almost anywhere in Iarrag. And after searching for decent amount of time, I found my way into the palace.

It was through one of the bathrooms. After attempting to get most of the sewer matter off of my body, I peeked outside the room. The halls were empty. If I was going to find the treasury, I needed to be fast, but very cautious. I went jogging down the corridor, asking myself where I would keep stashes of gold tiukes if I was a king in a castle. I figured if there was any, it would probably be near the top of the castle. I headed up a staircase slowly and silently. It was then that I began to notice that I had not seen anyone yet.

"Where is everyone?" I asked out loud.

I reached the top of the castle without meeting a single soul. I wasn't complaining, but it was just odd.

The treasury, however, eluded me. I couldn't find it anywhere. I opened door after door and found no treasure.

"Do they even have a treasury?" I groaned. Then I opened another door.

I knew right from the start that it was one of the royal's room. Everything in it was far too expensive for anyone who wasn't royalty. However, it was rather small. I usually assumed that royals would make enormous rooms for themselves, even if the room was only for one person.

This room was...too normal sized for royalty.

I let the thought drift away as I spotted a vanity in the corner of the room, next to a huge bookcase. Jewels and diamonds were laying on top of the vanity, along with a shining, very valuable-looking knife. I stepped in and shut the door behind me. I immediately put the jewels in my pack, but I took a moment to examine the knife. The sheath and handle were made of gold and were arrayed with beautiful, sparkling emeralds.

"Oh, that's a beauty." I laughed. I unsheathed it to see a long, very sharp blade.

I liked the knife. And I did need a new one. My last one had been used up gnawing through a tree trunk.

Then I heard the door open.

The door *opened*.

In my kind of business, speed and stealth were key. If you didn't have those attributes, you got caught rather quickly. Getting caught could sometimes mean death. Where I was, it most certainly would have meant death. Thankfully, I had spent a long time working on speed and stealth. My entire body was underneath the bed before the door was fully ajar.

"Stay here, Sophia." A guard told the princess. "Be safe. I put a knife on your vanity if you need it."

The knife that was now in my hands. Figures.

"Thank you, Jonathan." Princess Sophia replied.

The door shut again.

I sighed. *"They're really getting scared about me, huh?"*

I felt the mattress above me press down slightly. Princess Sophia was sitting down on her bed.

"Shepherd, please watch over us." She prayed.

I suddenly felt horrible. Princess Sophia was calling out to the Shepherd: the Creator of all that exists. The holy and righteous Judge.

The merciful and almighty God, the Lord of all lords, the King of all kings…

She was asking for His protection…because of me.

Let's face it, I was a miserable kind of person. A thief. A bandit. A criminal. But even *I* reverenced the Shepherd. And I felt convicted.

I let out a sigh, my conscience now burdening me.

Suddenly, I felt the mattress above me bounce slightly. A second after, Princess Sophia's face appeared. She was slightly hanging off her bed, looking underneath it to find me. In my surprise, I simply gaped at her. She returned the gaping look, mirroring the shock and fear that I was feeling. Princess Sophia let out the same small, scared-sounding gasp that she had when I was in the carriage.

"There's no way you heard that sigh." Was the only thing I could think to say.

"I did." She confessed in a shaky voice. "And it was the same one I heard in my father's carriage."

I blinked at her, surprised in so many ways.

"You have excellent hearing." I complimented.

"Thank you." She said, still looking terrified. Suddenly, her head whipped up from my view.

"Guards! Guards!" Sophia shrieked as she began bolting off of her bed. I, in turn, was scrambling from underneath her bed. Princess Sophia was running for the door. Luckily, I was faster than her. I grabbed her before she could reach the door. I clamped my hand over her mouth. She squirmed and continued to cry for the guards, but they were muffled.

For several moments, I held her there, listening if anyone was coming. Minutes passed. No guards came.

I relaxed somewhat. The princess had stopped screaming, but was still trying to break loose of my arms.

"Are you going to be quiet?" I asked calmly. "If you don't scream, I won't hurt you. Deal?"

She clutched my hand and thrusted it away from her.

"Let go of me!" She yelled. "Ugh! You stink!"

"Well, I should, because I got here through the sewers." I informed her. Princess Sophia immediately gave a foul expression of disgust.

"The SEWER?!" She gagged and desperately attempted to get the gunk off of her face that came from my hand.

"To be clear, though, I'm not here for 'revenge' as you and your father think." I explained, ignoring her moment of despair. "I'm not here to hurt anyone. I'm here for these."

I held up her jewels.

I suppose I expected the princess to react with accusations, confrontations, or…something like that.

But she didn't. In fact, she reacted quite differently than most people I robbed. She simply sat back on her bed with a look of quiet surprise and said:

"You're not here for me?"

I paused for a moment, distracted at her calm response. "No, I'm not."

"You're just here for money?" She nodded to her jewelry.

"Just enough for me and my raccoon." I told her as Korhn revealed himself by hobbling from under the bed.

I put the jewels back in my pack. "Oh, and this knife."

I showed her the knife. The one that the guard had left for her.

"Give me that! It's my friend's." Sophia demanded, reaching out for it. I pulled back out of her reach. "I *like* this knife. Besides, you owe me one for messing up my little raid on your father's carriage."

The princess humphed. "Well, you shouldn't steal."

"Some of us don't have much of a choice." I retaliated as Korhn hopped up my arm.

I turned to leave. Before I did, though, I said. "I'm sorry for scaring you and your father. I'm no assassin. Your lives were never in any danger."

"Well, you got in here, didn't you?" She pointed out. "And I've had a bad experience with a bandit before."

My ears perked up. I had heard of that story. "Well let me spare you from having another one. Goodbye."

I put my hand on the door latch.

"What's your name?"

I stopped. Somehow, that got to me. Rarely did people ask my name because rarely did anyone care. Rachel had been an exception, but it's one thing for any regular person to ask me…

It was another thing when royalty was asking me.

Never did I dream that a princess would care what my name was. I hesitated. I cleared my throat and turned around to her again.

"Why?" I asked, a little harshly. "So you can write it on the wanted posters?"

The princess seemed somewhat offended. "You are very rude, you know. I, a princess, asked you your name and you just spit back at me?"

I glared at her, but sighed and told her. "My name is Nathan."

"Nathan." Sophia tried it. "Where are your parents?"

A peculiar question to ask. I was older than she was.

"Dead."

Sophia's eyes softened. "Oh. I'm sorry."

I kept my glare. "Many are, but never enough to actually do something about it."

I could tell how my comment had hurt her. The pain was clear on her face. It only made me angrier. She had never faced the death of a loved one. She had never had to go a day without food.

Never had to become what everyone hated.

"I truly am sorry." She spoke very softly. "What would you wish for me to do?"

"I don't care." I replied, less harshly. "I've got what I need. Perhaps you could just say they fell down the gutter and save us both a lot of trouble."

I turned to leave, not actually thinking she would ever consider my request.

"I will." She replied.

I turned around to her again. "What?"

"I'll tell them the jewels you stole were simply lost." She explained to me.

I was confused. "Why?"

"Why not?" She countered, gently. "It's how I can help."

"You really want to help me?" I questioned.

"Yes." The princess nodded. "I've…seen what can drive a person to do insane, dangerous, and even wicked things. I'll help you this time."

I tried to see her angle. What would she benefit from doing this? I went over the scenarios in my mind and found…

Nothing.

I blinked. "Thank you."

She smiled back. "You're welcome."

I could see how she observed my eyes to the smallest aspect. It was like she was trying to read me, my thoughts, my feelings.

Either that, or she was just staring. After all, my eyes were silver. You don't see that every day.

Suddenly, the princess stood up off of her bed. She began to take steps toward me. She came within a short distance. With her hand, she reached up to my mask. Her eyes were filled with concern. She gently touched my mask with her hand.

"May I?" She asked in a soft whisper. I debated in my mind whether or not that was wise.

The logic within me knew it wasn't an option. Let the princess see my face? That was a ludicrous idea!

But, for some reason, I gave a small nod. She seemed so innocent and delicate. And beautiful. Hard to say no to a girl who looked like she had no evil in her heart, much less perform any evil. Her hand tightened on the mask and began to pull.

But the door burst open.

The door was directly behind me, so it plowed right into me and knocked me right into Princess Sophia. We both tumbled on the floor, Korhn falling on top of Princess Sophia. I instantly jumped back up, while Princess Sophia was just trying to figure out what had happened. A knight ran through the door. He had short brown hair and was very strongly built. He was clearly older than me, probably about two or three years older, but was short for his age. He actually was around my height, but I wasn't too tall for my age either.

"Princess, the Mirracians have taken the city! We must-" He stopped talking when he saw us.

It truly wasn't what it looked like, but it looked bad. I had a knife in my hand. The princess of Ferandar was lying on the floor at my feet.

"Uh, now, I know how this may seem, but-" I stuttered, immediately placing the knife in my pack.

"Get away from her!" The knight drew his sword and charged at me.

"No, Jonathan!" Sophia urged, still on the floor. Jonathan didn't listen. He was fast for a knight. He was on me within seconds. He brought his sword down, probably to split me in two. Before he could bring it down on me, though, I sidestepped it. Jonathan missed, thunking his sword onto the floor. I then thrusted my shoulder into his right side, catching him off-guard. He was knocked into the wall, trying to keep from completely falling over. Without any pause, I swung a wild fist right into his cheek. The punch had a good deal of force behind it, but it took two more to actually beat the guy to the ground. After he was well stunned, I kicked his sword away and ran for the door.

"Korhn, come." I called, lowering my arm. Korhn scurried off of Princess Sophia, leapt onto my arm, and climbed up onto my shoulder. I placed my hand on the latch, when the door flung open…*again*… and bashed me in the face.

I fell back on top of Jonathan. Korhn, however, was holding on tight and was still latched to my shoulder.

A gigantic, bald, black-bearded man came through the door. He was arrayed in dark red armor, the color of Mirrac. Old battle injuries covered his head. A seasoned warrior.

In his massive arms, he wielded a two-handed battle axe that had old, tribal markings carved into the helve.

I gasped at the sight of him and I froze. His piercing amber eyes seemed to dance with glee when he found the princess. His cruel smile showed an array of jagged teeth.

"I've found you, Princess." He smiled. Then his view turned to Jonathan and I.

He frowned. "A bandit?"

I was speechless. I was still in shock. Korhn violently hissed at him. The man's eyes then widened as he stared at me.

He was looking at my distinct, silver eyes. Shock and anger exploded on his face.

"*You*?! How?!" He growled fiercely.

"Leos!" I gasped, once I got my voice back.

Leos immediately swung his massive axe at me.

He was going to strike me down to kill me.

It wouldn't be the first time. I rolled, pulling Jonathan with me. Thanks to me, we were both able to dodge Leos' deadly blade. Once out of range, I leapt up on my feet as fast as I could. But Leos stayed, guarding the door.

Blocking my exit.

There was only one other place I could go. Princess Sophia's room had a balcony. I ran for it.

"Nathan, wait!" The princess pleaded.

"Thief!" Jonathan yelled, coming out of his daze.

Korhn screeched in fear, gripping my shoulder as tight as he could.

I pushed through the balcony doors.

I jumped over the balcony railing.

I began falling.

I was *really* high up. I was so high up that I could see far past the castle walls and over the nearest forest.

…And the army of Mirracians that were outside Iarrag and flooding into the city.

"*When did they get here?!*" I thought, watching the Mirracians as I was plummeting.

"*Oh, yeah. I'm falling.*" Was my next thought. "*Probably better do something about that.*"

My only chance at survival was grabbing onto something before I collided with the ground.

That something was a flag. It draped across the palace wall, underneath Sophia's room. I barely snatched onto it. Thankfully, it was made of strong stuff. It stopped my fall and I planted my feet against the wall. It was quite an exhilarating and terrifying experience. I was hanging high on a tower wall, kept from falling to my death by some thick fabric. Now that I was temporarily safe from sure death, I allowed myself to panic about Leos, who I had just seen in Sophia's room.

I had to get as far away from him as possible.

I glanced everywhere, urgently trying to find a way to safety. There had to be some way I could get down. Luckily, I was not too high up from a roof of another tower. I dropped and hit the roof hard, but nothing was broken.

I had to get out. I had to get out.

From that roof, I jumped to another building. I repeated this process one more time, fortunately with a building that was much closer to the ground. I was now away from the palace and closer to the marketplace. I slid down the side of the building to the ground. I very quickly ran inside a nearby house to evade Mirracian soldiers. They were everywhere.

If Leos was working with them, I wanted to be as far away from them, too. And judging by what Leos was wearing, there was a good chance he was now a Mirracian soldier.

I closed the door and waited there, breathing heavily. It was too dark for my eyes to see. They needed to adjust.

I was still a bit shaken. Korhn chattered next to me.

"Shh!" I hushed him. "I know it's Leos!"

I tried to calm myself down. I was freaking out at just the sight of him. I hadn't seen Leos in six years. The last time we saw each other, we were trying to kill one another.

Leos was a much better fighter than I. Still a much better fighter, probably.

I let out several deep breaths and finally calmed down enough. I cautiously opened the door. I only opened it an inch. I glanced out to find Mirracian soldiers coming closely within range. I shut the door again. I waited for a few moments for them to pass by. As I did, I rummaged through my pack. I snatched the sketch I had made a while back.

The drawing was of Leos. I stared at it for a moment. My art skills were awful. Plus, the sketch was very much outdated. I had drawn a young Leos. The Leos I had just seen had aged quite a bit.

I took a sigh before crumpling up the sketch and letting it fall to the floor.

I peeked outside again. No soldiers in sight this time. I checked for possible exits. I found out that we weren't too far from the city gate. As of right now, it wasn't really guarded by anyone. Both Iarrag soldiers and Mirracian soldiers were all fighting.

"If we can make it there, maybe we have a chance." I whispered to Korhn.

I was about to run out the door, when something hit me in the back of the head. Korhn began screeching as my vision faded.

"That's for ruining my bread." A voice echoed before I fell unconscious.

CHAPTER FOUR
AN UNUSUAL ESCAPE

I came to in a dark cell. It was quite strange. The cell seemed to be all wrong. The door to the cell was on the ceiling, and I seemed to be flying.

"What is this?" I asked groggily. I noticed there was no answer.

"*Where's Korhn?!*" I thought.

"Well, look who's finally awake." Jonathan said. I searched for where his voice came from.

"Over here." He said. I looked up. Jonathan was sitting in a jail cell on the ceiling.

"What is this place?" I asked in awe.

"A dungeon."

"This is the weirdest dungeon I've ever seen." I told him.

Jonathan sighed. "If you haven't figured it out yet, you're upside down."

I looked to my feet, and sure enough, I was tied with locked chains from the ceiling upside down. My hands were chained as well.

"Ah." I realized. "That's what it is."

I searched around the room again.

"What are you looking for?" Jonathan asked.

"Korhn." I answered.

"Corn? There's not going to be any corn down here. It's a dungeon."

"Not corn." I said. "Korhn, my raccoon."

"Oh," He realized. "He's upstairs, along with King William, Queen Terra, and Princess Sophia."

"What?" I asked.

"They're holding Queen Terra and Princess Sophia hostage so King William will agree to whatever the Mirracian king wants." He grumbled. "And this was all because of you, Thief."

"The thief who saved your sorry rump from a madman's axe." I muttered.

Apparently, Jonathan didn't hear me. He turned away from me. "You bandits are all the same."

"Well, just blame it all on me." I said sarcastically. "Don't blame it on the man who waged war on you and sent the soldiers to take over your Nation. No, blame the penniless thief."

"Just be quiet, will you?" He glanced over his shoulder. "Or how about this? Find a way to get us out of here."

I squinted at him. "Is that a challenge?"

"Nevermind." He muttered.

"Well, I accept your challenge." I said confidently.

He turned to me. "What?"

"I'm going to get you out." I replied. "Just like you asked me to."

He scoffed "How can you get me out? You're chained upside down."

"Which is a bit overkill, if you ask me." I muttered under my breath. Jonathan, however, was still talking, actually. He apparently detested thieves. He was going on about how thieves are nothing but selfish, moronic, low-lives and blah, blah, blah. As he kept going on and on about how I would never be able to escape, I started swinging.

"I mean this is-" Suddenly he stopped and looked at me.

"What are you doing?" Jonathan asked. I ignored him and swung myself upward so I could reach my belt. In my belt was my pick. I pulled it out with my teeth, and began to maneuver my chained hands to where I could unlock them. To finagle chained hands from behind your back to your front alone is truly difficult. But, if you practice some, it can become manageable.

But it tends to hurt. I wouldn't recommend it if you don't have to. First, I tested the chains, seeing how tight they really were around my wrists. Snug, but not too tight. I took a moment to shake the chains up past my wrists, then turned in my left arm and pulled it up to form a small triangle that I could fit my head through. It put incredible strain on my shoulder, and if I did it wrong, I would dislocate my shoulder. And that would be painful.

I've heard that many people can't do it the way I do, but that's thanks to the way my body was built. After some moments, my chained hands were in front of me and I was able to start working on the lock with my pick.

I won't even start on how hard it is to unlock something when the pick is in your mouth.

Jonathan was quiet while I did all of this. Probably shamed into silence.

After I got my hands free, I used them to work on the lock that was attached to my feet. As I did this, I snickered.

"It seems the thief isn't as dumb as he looks." I laughed. After I said this, the chains unlocked. Which means they were no longer holding me in the air. So, I fell.

"Wah!" I screamed and landed with a very hard, painful thud. Right on my back.

"Oh, no. Not at all." Jonathan chuckled sarcastically.

"Ugghh." I moaned as stood to my feet. Jonathan was smirking.

"Oh yeah?" I pointed at him while in pain. "Let's see *you* get out of that."

"All right, I admit it." Jonathan confessed. "I would have never gotten out of that. Now, get me out of here. We need to help the royal family."

"Okay, I'll be right there." I said regaining strength as I cracked my back. "But I want a full pardon if I help you."

"Done." Jonathan promised.

I unlocked my door, then Jonathan's.

"One problem." Jonathan pointed out. "We don't have any weapons."

"No." I agreed. "But we do have the element of surprise. We're going to give a little something they won't be expecting."

Jonathan raised an eyebrow. I pulled up my mask.

The entrance of the dungeon was guarded by two Mirracian guards. Fortunately, they didn't expect us to get out of the cells. From what I could hear through the door, they seemed to be having lunch. I told Jonathan what to do as I climbed up above the door. When I was ready, Jonathan threw a rock at the door. The guards got up and opened the door to see what was going on. While they came in to find nothing out of the ordinary, I swung down from the ceiling and kicked them both down the stairs. When the both fell to the bottom, Jonathan came out, took their swords, and knocked them both out. We stripped them of their armor and threw them in the dungeon. Disguised as Mirracian soldiers, with armor that was too big for us, we began to make our way to the throne room without any confrontation from anyone.

Jonathan gulped nervously.

"What's the matter, Jon?" I asked with a laugh. "No one recognizes us. Just act like you know what you're doing."

"But I don't know what I'm doing!" He whispered nervously. "I don't know where anything is!"

I stopped walking. "What? What do you mean you don't know where anything is? You're a palace knight, aren't you?"

He stopped a little further away. He was sweating. "Yes, but I don't know where anything is because we are in Lasónay. Not Iarrag."

Iarrag was the Ferandaron capitol.

Lasónay was the Mirracian capitol.

"Oh, stop." I laughed, thinking he was joking.

Jon stared at me gravely.

I blinked. "You can't be serious. It's impossible. I was only out for a couple hours."

"No." Jon shook his head nervously. "You've been unconscious for the whole trip."

I was starting to get worried. "How could I have been out for the whole trip from Ferandar to Mirrac? That's nearly a week of travel!"

"Seth's assassin gave you some sort of…elixir every so often to keep you from waking."

"What? But that means…Why didn't you tell me?!" I looked around nervously. "We have got to get out of here!"

I began to run, when Jon grabbed my armored shoulder.

"Not without the royal family, Thief!"

I shoved him off of me. "Are you insane?! We can't escape with them! This is Mirrac! They have miles of territory! The second largest Nation! Even if we went without the royal family we would have very slim to no chances! They probably know we escaped from the dungeon already!"

"How would they know that?" Jon questioned.

I threw my arms open, showing the Mirracian armor that we stole. It clearly did not fit. "Would you be able to tell who was a guard in Iarrag if he wore armor that didn't fit?"

Jon paused and then sighed.

"My loyalty is to the royal family of Ferandar. They need my help, but I need your help to save them. Will you help me…Please?"

I didn't want to. I *really* didn't want to.

But it was the right thing to do.

"Uggh…" I groaned, shaking my head. "How do you expect us to make this jail break?"

49

He thought on that. "I…was, uh-"

I complained. "You have no plan."

"We'll why don't you come up with something?"

"I don't know anything about castles!"

"You broke into Iarrag pretty easily." Jon pointed out.

"Still not a good idea to put me in charge of this rescue!"

Suddenly, we both stopped bickering to notice a Mirracian woman with a basket of flowers standing just down the hall, with a wide-eyed expression.

"Uh…Hello." Jonathan waved with a smile.

"Guards! Guards! Come help!" She shrieked. We both nearly tackled into her in order to cover her mouth.

"Mmmf! MMMMFF!!" She desperately tried to say.

"Look, look!" I explained. "We don't want any other trouble."

She began to calm down.

"Unhand her, you dogs!" Someone yelled behind us. We both turned around. It was only one guard, his sword drawn.

"We can take him." Jon said to me. However, the guard took a horn that was at his belt and sounded it. Much more Mirracians would be coming soon.

"Probably not the best idea." I replied to Jon. "Run!"

We both took off, leaving the woman behind. I ran down the right hallway while Jon took the left. Before long, guards were catching onto my trail. I wasn't as fast in heavy armor and I was very noticeable. About twenty or so guards were following me. I sprinted down the hall, not knowing where I was going, until I couldn't hear the guards any more. I found a door, opened it, and ran inside.

"Whew!" I sighed in relief. Then I happened to notice where I was. I was in a banqueting hall. And apparently, it seemed to be lunch time. Guards, archers, axemen, and spearmen stared at me. The longer I stood there, the more guards would stare at me, and the quieter it became throughout the room. What I also noticed is that warriors of the castle need to be ready at any moment for battle…which means they ate with their weapons at their side. They all saw what I was wearing and immediately knew that I was not a Mirracian guard. They began glaring at me and clutching their weapons.

"Oh." Was all I said before I rushed back out the door. I heard them yelling and running for the door behind me. I ran further down the hall, when I found Jonathan.

"Don't worry! We lost them!" He beamed.

"Speak for yourself!" I screamed as I passed him. He glanced down the hall.

"Oh my goodness!"

I ignored him and began to ditch the guard armor. The more I got rid of, the faster I could run. Jon caught up beside me, doing the same.

"We can't outrun them for long! What are we going to do?"

"Find the sewers!" I yelled. Suddenly, an arrow whizzed past me. Some archers were firing. During all of this running, I had realized that Jon and I ran back the way we came. I saw the dungeon door on the right. It was a huge door, built to keep the strongest of men in. With a giant lock that only one key could unlock. Fortunately, when we took out the guards, I stole the key.

Force of habit.

I pulled up my mask.

"This way!" I told him. We ran through the door.

"What now?" Jon asked, frantically. "We have nowhere to go!"

I was hoisting myself up the walls above the door. Right hand and foot pushing against the right wall, left hand and foot pushing against the left wall.

"What are you doing?" Jon asked.

"Climb, idiot!"

"They'll see us up there!"

"You got a better idea?!"

Jon quickly hoisted himself up above the door alongside me. A second after he did, the door slammed open, the warriors swarming in.

Without looking up, they immediately went down the stairs, expecting to find two intruders hiding down there. They stopped, realizing that we were suddenly gone. There was no one besides the two guards in a cell.

"Where'd they go?"

"They couldn't have just disappeared."

"They're not here, though." Were the random comments.

Jon and I dropped down.

"Ahem!" I cleared my throat. They all turned around to find me and Jonathan in the dungeon doorway.

"What the?!"

"Get 'em!" They all screamed. Unfortunately for them, we closed the door and locked it.

Jonathan laughed. "They didn't see that coming!"

"People don't usually look up." I commented as the soldiers began to bang on the door. "And you said it wouldn't work."

"It was close." Jon chuckled.

"Yeah, it was." I cleared my throat again. "But now we need to get back to business."

Jon became serious "So you're going to help me?"

I looked around frequently for any other guards. "Yeah. But I still want that pardon."

"Right, so what's the plan?" He asked.

I thought for a bit. "Well, we need to be stealthy. Undetected is always good. Let's see...There's going to be well trained soldiers because they *really* don't want the royal family to escape."

"Unless Lord Seth is over-confident." Jon mentioned.

"Is he the type?" I asked.

"From what I've heard."

"Okay, but let's just assume he's going on the safe side today. We'll need a diversion to get most of the guards out of there. Probably you, because you're more of a threat."

Jon smirked.

"With the guards gone, I'll get the royal family out of there. Then, we'll hide for a couple of days, and when they start sending out men to look for us, we just hitch a ride home."

I felt like it was a fantastic plan.

He looked at me, skeptically. "That's, uh, quite a plan you got there."

I gave him a blank expression. "Come on, I've done stuff like this a thousand of times."

"It has a lot of…holes."

"So we improvise." I replied. "It always works for me."

Jon gave me a skeptical look. "You got caught twice in Iarrag."

"Hey! I still made it to the Princess's room." I pointed out.

Then I stopped and thought of that situation. "And so we're clear, I wasn't trying to kill her. I was trying to steal these."

I went to grab the jewels in my pack, but nothing was in there. I gasped. "They stole the jewels I stole!"

"Oh, how evil." Jon rolled his eyes. "Yes, they took everything of worth off your person on the way over here."

The words 'on the way over here' seemed to echo in my head. "And I was out for all of that because of Leos' elixir?"

Jon nodded. "I'm betting he's a witch."

I couldn't help but laugh at that. "No, he's not a witch. But this sleep potion is interesting. Wait, what about my knife? They took that too?"

"You mean *my* knife?" Jon eyed me. "The one you took from Sophia?"

"Does Lord Seth have it?"

"How should I know?" Jon shrugged. "It's a good bet, though. It was a gift from King William himself."

"Well, I would very much like it back."

"Nathan. It's *my* knife."

I hung from an awning near the ceiling of the throne room. I was able to sneak through a high window. Still, getting up there without being seen was a true miracle. I was watching below as Lord Seth of the kingdom of Mirrac was working out everything he wanted from King William and his kingdom. About a dozen guards stood between the large door and the royal family. William was reading a treaty. No doubt one that would provide Mirrac with an unconditional surrender from Ferandar. With that, Seth would be able to take whatever he wanted from the land of Ferandar: trade, wealth, weapons, people. Why, he could even make Ferandar a part of Mirrac. From the awning I was hanging from, I climbed onto a near chandelier to see better. Princess Sophia and her mother, the queen of Ferandar, were seated in nearby chairs. To ensure King William would sign the treaty, several guards with swords surrounded the queen and the princess. In Sophia's hands was Korhn. She petted him delicately, and Korhn loved it. He snuggled in her arms, even with all the guards around them. Sophia seemed calm also. I noticed that she was still in the beautiful white dress. Now was the perfect moment for Jon to make his entry. I chose a large pebble from my boot and hurled it at the door. When it made contact, a loud thud rang throughout the throne room. Guards peered at the door curiously, and one guard reached for the door when it suddenly burst open with Jonathan at the entrance. He quickly knocked the soldier to the ground that answered the door.

"Lord Seth of Mirrac! Prepare for your doom!" Jon shouted and unsheathed his sword.

I chuckled. "*What an idiot.*"

Lord Seth simply gave Jonathan an annoyed, but puzzled stare. He snapped his fingers and several guards instantly ran to attack Jonathan. Jonathan took off with some of the soldiers chasing after him, all except the ones guarding the princess and queen. I smirked.

"*Easy.*" I thought and leaped from the chandelier. Before hitting the ground, I grabbed onto a Mirracian banner and slipped down the long cloth. All eyes turned to my masked face.

Sophia gasped. This time, it had a hint of excitement in it.

"Hi." I grinned under my mask.

I jumped from the banner and kicked two of the guards in the face. The next nearest one swung his sword at me and was surprised when I easily avoided it. I kicked him between the knees and took his sword from him. He instantly let go and I used the hilt of the sword to knock him unconscious. Five more swordsmen stood before me.

Big. Slow. Easy to make them get in each other's way.

Before long, they were dealt with. I had taken care of eight guards of Mirrac without receiving one scratch from them.

I had a little bit of pride in my step after that. Especially after seeing the royals' looks of amazement. With their amazement came some other emotions: For Sophia, she was also happy. The only one who was. William and Terra had grown pale. Seth, along with calm surprise, had a face of intrigue and curiosity.

I smiled anyway. I held out my arm and Korhn leaped up on it from Princess Sophia's arm. He climbed up onto my shoulder.

"Princess." I bowed. "We haven't much time. Get your parents, we'll get Jon, and get out of here."

Sophia nodded quickly and took her mother's hands to follow me out the door. King William, however, seemed insulted.

"How dare you! You don't speak to my daughter that way! The **king's** daughter! You forget your place, Thief!"

"I did bow." I defended. "Plus, this thief just saved you and your family. If you wish to stay and wait for the soldiers to come back, be my guest."

King William decided to join us. Lord Seth remained deathly silent. He sat down at his throne and put his hands together right below his nose, making him look like he was in deep thought. He knew he had been defeated (by a thief) and accepted it. We were about to leave the room, when I saw something next to Lord Seth's throne. I ran back and snatched the emerald knife.

"This is mine." I smirked at Seth.

For a moment, Seth had a bewildered and confused look.

It was as if he recognized my face, or at least the part of my face that was shown. Then the expression was gone.

He sat there as I ran back and joined the others.

We ran out of the throne room to find Jon outside the door. When he saw the royal family, he bowed low.

"Your majesties." He spoke humbly.

"Ah, Jonathan." King William smiled. "Finally, someone with respect to his rulers. Not like this scum."

"Seriously, I *bowed*." I said again. "Why is his bow better than mine?"

"Do you know your way out of here?" Queen Terra asked Jon.

Jon gulped. "I don't. Do you? Surely Lord Seth had you walk through here."

"Our transport didn't have windows." Princess Sophia told us. "And this palace is like a maze."

I began chuckling. "We-heh-ell, looks like you four are in a bit of a fix, aren't you?"

"You know you're way around here?" Jon raised a suspicious eyebrow at me.

I smiled. "I know *a* way. And it will keep us completely undetected. You can join me, but I guarantee you won't like it."

They didn't like it.

It was in the sewers.

"This is revolting!" The queen shouted at me as we descended down a toilet gutter. "Why are we trusting him anyway?!"

I was getting very sick of everyone treating me like scum. I was ready to leave them, but Princess Sophia was the only thing keeping me around.

"Mother, please." She reasoned with the queen. "It's better than being prisoners. He is helping us. He saved us."

Queen Terra muttered under her breath, not being able to argue against the fact that I had indeed saved them. I then pondered why the princess seemed to be on my side. She had only insulted me once. From then on, she was trying to help me.

Due to the first time we met, I strongly trusted that she would rather be a prisoner than be in this slime pit. I could tell by her face and the way she held her breath. They all did that. Only Korhn and I breathed normally.

It's not that I was used to sewer smell, it's just that I grew up being able to deal with foul smells.

They had not, being raised to have anything they desired.

King William gave some complaints as well, but Princess Sophia hushed him also. She gave him reason to trust me, though I believed that he was beginning to realize that I was the same thief that had been in his carriage. I tried to hide my eyes from him, but he kept trying to get a closer look.

That's what I get for having silver eyes.

I reached an exit to the sewer. I glanced out to see we had made it outside the castle walls. Beyond us were farmlands and, past those, forest area. But just to be safe, I sent Korhn to peer through the drain. He screeched back to me.

I immediately stopped everyone.

"What is it?" Jonathan questioned.

"Korhn says we can't go yet." I answered.

The king, queen, and Jon gave me a look like I was crazy. The princess gave me the same look, but it somehow seemed less insulting.

"The fumes must've gotten to your head, boy." The king glared. "Now you can talk to your rat?"

I was ready to just hand over the king to Mirracians. I was thinking over that Seth might've given me safe passage if I did.

"He's not a rat." I corrected quietly. "He is a raccoon."

"Looks like a rodent." The king sneered. "I see little difference."

"It's fatter than a rat." The queen commented.

I turned to them and pointed an accusing finger at him.

"Listen, you!" I whispered violently. "I've about had it! One more remark like that and I will personally hand you over to Seth!"

"You will not, Thief!" Jonathan defended, reaching for his sword.

I glared at him, but I held my tongue. I had a little respect for Jonathan. Jonathan's hand was still on his sword and the air grew very tense. Until Princess Sophia stepped in.

"Perhaps we have been a bit rude to our rescuer." Princess Sophia stated quietly. For some reason, when I heard her speak in such a soft tone in my favor, I calmed down.

I wasn't used to someone defending me.

Her statement also made Jonathan step back and release his grip on his sword.

King William and Queen Terra became silent.

I then thought about what I had just said. I had threatened to throw them to the Mirracians. Sure, I was their rescuer, but I was talking to royalty. William was too proud to let anyone talk to him like that. He would have me hanged as soon as he was safe. I pondered over this.

"I need you to promise me something." I told King William.

He gave me a sneer. "Tiukes. Of course. You thieves are all the same."

"Just can't stop, can you?" I groaned. "No, I don't want money. I want your word of honor that when we return safely to Ferandar, I will be pardoned for all I have said and done against you and your family."

King William stared at me for a moment. "If you get me and my family home safely, then I will grant you what you have asked."

"Good enough." I replied. I held out my hand to seal the deal, but the king did not reach out for my hand.

"You're not going to shake my hand?" I questioned. "It's to make it a real accord."

"My word should be enough." He said coldly.

I lowered my hand. "Fine then. Korhn?"

Korhn chattered back. I nodded.

"Okay, it's clear." I told them. "Let's go."

They all gave me skeptical looks, but after seeing that I hopped out of the drain, plus their disgust of the sewers, they followed.

Being outside, there weren't many places to hide. Many of the guards were still looking for us elsewhere, not expecting us to get this far.

But that did not mean we were safe yet. We quickly made our way to some heavy brush. I stopped everyone before going out in the open.

There was a large stable just several yards away, with ready horses and carriages.

But also multiple guards. I counted twelve.

Jon came up to me. "We're stealing their carriages?"

I grinned under my mask. "You expect us to walk?"

Then I turned to the rest. "Okay, Jon, you get the royal family to a carriage and get the horses."

They all seemed to understand. I turned to Korhn.

"Korhn, you go with them and keep them safe." I whispered to him.

Korhn wanted to go with me. He began arguing with me.

"No." I said firmly. "I need you to watch over them. They have a habit of running into trouble. I'll be okay."

That seemed to get him. He agreed.

"What about you?" King William asked suddenly. "Are you going to defeat the guards? Or just leave us to them?"

"How about you take a leap of faith and trust me?" I countered back and before he could reply with any other insult, I ran out. I snuck behind the stables and climbed up to the top of it. I jumped to a ledge and crawled across to where I was right over the soldiers.

I nodded to Jon and dove off my perch. I fell and thrusted my legs down right on top of one of the guards. He was down. The others instantly noticed me and took out their weapons. I threw a punch at the first and knocked him back a ways. Then I took off, knowing they would follow. As they did, I could see Jon rushing the royal family to a carriage out of the corner of my eye. Korhn was perched on Princess Sophia's shoulder. I made sure to lead the guards away far enough.

I ran down a dirt path out into a nearby wood.

My domain.

We were far enough. I spun around and attacked one of the guards. I tackled into him and rolled across the dirt floor. We rolled down a steep hill and, all the way, I was beating him maliciously. The others ran after us, but when I got up, I used the soldier as a shield. The soldier was much too worn out to actually fight anymore, so I just threw him around, protecting myself with him. Finally, I threw him at one of the guards. As the guards were preoccupied with helping their fallen friend, I attacked again. I kicked one guard between the legs, which took him down in an instant. I then leapt up and kicked two other guards in the face. As I fell onto the ground, the rest of the

guards tried to impale me with their weapons. One actually got part of my cloak. I spun on my back and tripped three of them with my legs. As they fell, I jumped back up. But now, the guards were beginning to overwhelm me. Four more ran at me with swords. I had no choice but to take out my knife. I blocked one guard's sword, but others still came at me. I tried dodging their weapons, but one slashed across my arm. "Gah!" I yelped and put my hand on the bleeding wound.
I put down my guard.
Huge mistake.
Four swords slashed at me. One nicked my chest. Another cut a slash in my stomach. I managed to dodge the other two, but I was wounded. My stomach was already bleeding. I was in trouble. I knew it. The guards knew it. They knew I wouldn't be able to last much longer.
I had no choice.
I skillfully threw my knife right into the throats of one of the soldiers. Then, without hesitation, I ran full-force at the other three. I threw myself right into them and knocked them all down. Fortunately, they were surprised that I would take such a risk, and therefore, weren't prepared.
As we all fell, I stole one of the soldier's swords and did what I had to with it. I swung it at all of them. I didn't want to, but it was either their lives or mine.
Before long, they were all dead.
I stopped after they were all motionless, not breathing.
I looked at my hands.
Covered in blood.
I let out a deep sigh. Death was not foreign to me, but I was never the one who brought it. I walked over to the guard that had my knife in his neck and removed it.
I stepped away from the dead bodies.
I had to go. I couldn't stay.
I turned and ran back to the gates.

SOPHIA

We waited for Nathan to return for a while. I gently pet his raccoon in my arms.

"Jonathan, go." My father ordered suddenly. "We need to get out of here."

"But Father, what about Nathan?" I asked him. "We need to wait for him to come back."

"We're leaving now." My father replied.

"No, Father!" I pleaded. "We can't! Not yet!"

"Sophia!" My mother snapped at me. "Silence yourself!"

I didn't listen to her. I grabbed my father's arm. "Father, he saved us! We need to wait!"

"No, Sophia." My father told me, not even looking at me. "The thief did help us, but we can't allow him to come with us. He's probably dead by now anyway."

"If I may, sir." Jonathan spoke from the front of the carriage we sat in. "He's quite clever. He won't be dead."

"I don't care!" My father suddenly shouted. "I'll not risk my family for a thief! We leave now! Drive, Jonathan!"

"Yes, my king." Jonathan obeyed and snapped the reins. The horses began moving at a fast pace.

"Father, we can't leave him!" I reasoned.

"Sophia, hush!" My mother whispered angrily at me.

My father pointed a finger at me. "That's enough out of you! If you remember right, you'll realize that this thief stole from us and would have taken you captive if he had the chance! Don't you remember the last thief you encountered?"

I shut my mouth. I did remember. My father continued.

"I'll not endanger our lives by waiting for a filthy thief just because you've fallen under some charm of his!"

My father turned and sat back in his seat. That meant that the subject was finished. I was not to bring it up again. We rode with Lasónay sinking into the distance. As Jonathan began pushing the horses to run faster, I thought on what my father said.

"Fallen under some charm?" I thought to myself. *"Have I?"*

I remembered when I first met Nathan. I was terrified. The second meeting, I was disgusted.

The third…

Excited?

But was that because I liked him? Was that because I had grown some feeling for him? No. Of course not.

However…

I shoved the thought away. It could be dealt with at another time.

"Wait!" A voice called from behind the carriage.

I gasped with delight. Korhn's head shot up. We both knew that voice! My father, Korhn, and I immediately looked out the window.

Sure enough, Nathan was running behind us, trying to catch up. Korhn began screeching.

"Stop the carriage, Jonathan!" I ordered.

"Do not stop this carriage!" My father yelled.

Jonathan obeyed and kept the horses running at full speed.

Nathan noticed.

"You lying wretch!" He shouted at my father.

My father just smirked to himself and sat back in his seat. I knew I could not argue with him anymore. I looked back out the window, hoping that Nathan would still escape okay. Korhn kept screeching at him.

I became a little discouraged as I watched Nathan shrink away.

Will I ever see him again? I asked myself.

Then I saw something else. I squinted to see what it was.

Horses. Mirracian soldiers were riding out to catch us.

"Jonathan, speed up the horses!" I shouted.

My father heard me and glanced out the window. He saw the horses.

"They're trying to catch us!" He gasped. "Jonathan, go faster!"

"I can't, sir!" He told us. "They're running at full speed!"

I began to worry. Nathan had probably been killed by them and now they were coming for us. Then I squinted again. One of the guards… looked different.

Korhn screeched happily. I smiled with glee.

Nathan had stolen one of the horses and was riding to us. Nathan was zipping past the Mirracian soldiers like an arrow. I marveled at how he was able to urge his horse on so much faster than the others.

He rode up to the carriage and glared at my father angrily.

"Some agreement!" He raged.

My father remained silent. I noticed that Nathan was bleeding badly. He had a bad slash across his stomach.

"Nathan!" I called to him. "You're bleeding!"

"I'm aware!" He responded as Korhn jumped out of the carriage onto Nathan's shoulder.

"Nathan, those Mirracian soldiers are gaining on us!" Jonathan yelled to Nathan as he snapped the reigns again. "I need you to stop them!"

Nathan glanced back at the soldiers getting closer.

"Okay. I'll do what I can." He said.

"What?" Jonathan yelled. The wind was really making it hard to hear.

"I SAID 'OKAY'!" Nathan shouted

Then he started riding back towards the other horsemen.

"Your majesties!" Jonathan yelled to us. "I ask that you get down and shelter yourselves! They may catch us soon!"

My mother and father immediately did as Jonathan asked, but I wasn't going to hide like a helpless girl. I refused to. Instead of getting down and bury myself under blankets and armor, I reached for the door and climbed out.

"Sophia!" My parents called after me. I didn't listen to them. I didn't turn back. I hoisted myself onto the side of the carriage and mounted up to the front where Jonathan was.

Jonathan must have thought I was a Mirracian. He was about to shove me off when he recognized me.

"Princess?!" He gaped. "What in blazes are you doing up here?!"

"Give me your sword!" I commanded.

"Princess, I-" He began to say.

"Give! Me! Your sword!" I shouted angrily.

He seemed surprised at how forceful I was. He unsheathed his sword and handed it to me. I then scaled onto the back of the carriage and readied myself.

The Mirracian riders were closer than ever now. Nathan and Korhn were holding off a few. Nathan was riding up and slashing the horses at the legs so the horse would either tumble over or just stop. Not something I would have ever thought about doing. I loved animals. I didn't want to see them hurt, but I understood why he did it. It was so that even if the rider was pushed off, he couldn't get back on his horse. Korhn was on top of a Mirracian horseman, scratching at his face. Still, riders were reaching the carriage. They had slipped past Nathan. Two jumped onto the carriage and hoisted themselves up to where I was. I held Jonathan's sword ready. The first came up.

"Lower your weapon!" He shouted at me.

"No!" I replied defiantly.

He sneered at me and then lifted his sword. My father made sure I was put through sword training. I remembered the teaching that I had been given. I parried his sword and swung my blade at him, but the soldier dodged my strike. It seemed to be child's play for him.

"Now, now, little girl." He grinned. "I don't want to hurt you."

I thrusted my sword at him, but he easily sidestepped it. I became a little worried.

"Just put it down, tell your driver to stop and you won't be harmed." He told me.

My mind raced. *"What am I going to do?!"*

I lowered my sword. "Okay."

The soldier smiled. He lowered his weapon. "Now tell your driver to stop."

I was about to do it. I had given up, when I saw a window of opportunity.

The soldier turned to see his other comrade climbing up. He was distracted.

My eyes widened when I saw it. I ran up and kicked the soldier. He tumbled off the carriage, knocking the other soldier with him. They rolled along the dirt road.

I jumped up and down, feeling the success run through me. Suddenly, I felt a tap on my shoulder.

A soldier! I spun around and slapped the man behind me.

It was Nathan.

"Oh! Nathan!" I gasped as I reached to him to keep him from falling off the carriage. The slap knocked him far back enough.

"I'm so sorry!" I apologized.

He groaned a bit. "There's this thing called an ally. Slapping is rather looked down upon concerning them."

"I'm sorry! I thought you were a Mirracian!" I defended.

Nathan shrugged it off. Then he looked past me, his eyes very serious. I turned to see what he was looking at. More riders were coming. Nathan took out his knife.

"Can you use that?" He asked me, nudging towards Jonathan's sword.
I smirked. "Of course. I'll have you know I took out two soldiers."
Nathan laughed underneath his mask. "After you surrendered."
I frowned. "You saw that?"
"Pay attention." He ordered. "They're coming."
I turned back to see that the riders were already jumping onto the carriage and climbing up. Nathan ran kicked one off that was getting on top. I joined in. I ran to one and slashed his hand. He yelped and fell to the ground. I noticed that the ride on top of the carriage was getting bumpier. I looked and saw we were now on a much rougher road. Jonathan kept the horses going at full speed.
While I was distracted, a soldier came up behind me and grabbed me. I began shrieking and yelling for Nathan to help me. Nathan was preoccupied with fighting two other soldiers.
"Sophia!" He yelled, not being able to get to me.
"Nathan! Nathan! Help!" I screamed. The soldier was dragging me to the edge of the carriage.
"Dear goodness! Is he really thinking about jumping off?!" I screamed in my head.
Sure enough, he was. He was about to, when Jonathan grabbed a hold of him. The two struggled and the soldier let go of me. I fell on the carriage and watched as Jonathan jumped around the soldier and put him in a choke hold. As the soldier struggled to get free, Jonathan then tossed him off of the carriage. Nathan had also dealt with the two other soldiers. He turned to Jonathan.
"Nice save." Nathan commented. Then fear came to his eyes. "Jon? Who's driving?"
We all turned to see no one driving. The horses were coming to a sharp turn, still going at full speed. They turned, but it was still too sharp. The carriage broke away from the horses and tumbled down a steep hill.
With all of us on top.

...I was hurt. Badly. I was also disoriented. Things were blurry. I couldn't seem to hear anything. I tried to stand up, but something kept me down. Then I began to hear something.
"So-!" A voice called. It was very distant.
"So-!" "-ia!"

It started to become clearer. Someone was calling my name. I tried to get up again.

No luck. I was sure. Something was on top of me.

I was beginning to see again. Someone was in front of me.

"Nathan?" I asked.

The figure didn't respond. I tried to focus.

The figure looked like it lifting something up.

A sword?

Then another figure came and shoved him. A struggle happened then, but the second figure overcame the other.

He was the one who kept yelling my name.

I squinted. A dark green cloaked figure.

Nathan.

He crawled closer to me. Why was he crawling?

He was inches away from my face. I could see his masked face clearly.

"Sophia!" He yelled. His yell was so faint. So quiet.

Why was it so quiet? Was my hearing going away?

Suddenly, Nathan's face was gone. Then I felt the weight of the thing that was on top of me begin to lift.

What was happening?

"Get her out!" Nathan's voice called faintly. "It's crushing her!"

I felt strong arms grab a hold of my body. I felt them pull me and I was being dragged across the grass. Something on the grass was wet.

Surely not water. Everything was too confusing. I couldn't make anything out of it.

Then, we were running. I was being carried. It was either Nathan or Jonathan that was carrying me. I kept asking where my mother was. I could hear every now and then:

"I'm right here, dear. I'm right here."

Then something happened. A lot of screaming. A lot of shouting. Swords flashing. Cries of pain.

Then, falling. I felt myself rolling down a steep hill. I landed in something soft.

Very soft….and cold.

I was in water. I tried to swim, but I was wounded further than I thought.

I could barely move correctly. I noticed that I needed air, and without thinking properly, I tried to suck in air.

I sucked in water. I began choking and tried to reach the surface.
I was dying. I was dying!
And there was nothing I could do about it…
Nothing I could do about it…
Dying…
My father, my mother. I wouldn't ever see them again.
That last thing I said to my father…So foolish of me. But then I felt myself rising.
I burst through the surface and was thrown onto the shore. I was breathing, I was on ground.
I was going to live.

CHAPTER FIVE
ALONE WITH A PRINCESS

NATHAN

Princess Sophia began to wake. She opened her eyes and slowly sat upright.

"How are you feeling?" I asked her, completely exhausted. I was about to collapse. Fortunately, a tree was holding me up, helping me sit upright to stoke the fire. I had helped the royal family escape, distracted the guards so Jonathan could get them in a wagon, fought the horse riders, fallen down the hill with the carriage, lifted the carriage off of Princess Sophia as Jonathan dragged her out, ran from the Mirracian soldiers in the forest, fought off the soldiers, fell off the steep cliff into a lake with Sophia, and saved Sophia from drowning. Not only that, but I had been wounded nearly the entire time.

I...was...exhausted.

The princess had been unconscious for a couple hours. The sun was starting to get low in the sky. Princess Sophia glanced around slowly.

"What happened?" She asked groggily.

"After we fell down the hill with the carriage, we had to run from the Mirracians. You and I fell down a cliff into that lake."

I pointed across to the lake. She gazed at it.

"Then I helped you out and treated your injuries." I explained as I finished treating my own wounds. "Oh yes, I also got a couple fish. Would you care for one?"

I held out a fried fish that I had just cooked in the fire. She stared at it for the longest time. Then her eyes widened.

"No! That poor fish!" She gasped. "That's so terrible of you!"

I brought the fish back. "I guess not."

Sophia began to fully wake up. She looked around anxiously.

"Where are my parents?! Where's Jonathan?!" She asked, quite worried.

"Relax, relax." I tried to calm her. I reached out and put my hand on her shoulder.

She was breathing pretty fast.

"Princess! Calm down." I shook her a bit with my hand.

She turned to face me. She stared right into my eyes and she slowly began to calm.

It actually crept me out. She was going back into the trance-like state that I had seen earlier.

"Okay." She whispered, staring at me.

I got the feeling that she was beginning to get attached to me. I took my hand off her shoulder.

"We got separated." I explained as I turned back to cooking the fish. "Jonathan is with your parents. They'll be fine with him."

Sophia broke out of her trance. "Yes, you're right. They'll be fine." She glanced at the pile of fish. "Is there anything besides fish?"

I gave her a questioning look. "You got a grudge against meat?"

She shook her head. "No, I eat meat all the time. It's just...I don't eat anything that *looks* like an animal."

I was confused. "What?"

She tried to explain. "I love animals, see? I will eat beef, but I don't want it to look like a cow. Does that make sense? I'll eat fish, but I can't when it *looks* like fish."

Then I understood. "Ohhh. Okay. You don't want to think that you're eating an animal."

She nodded. "Yes, that's it."

I shook my head. "That is amazing."

"Oh, thank you." Sophia smiled.

"That wasn't a compliment." I told her. "But it looks like you'll be fine. I sent Korhn to go find some fruit."

Then I heard rustling through the trees.

"Speak of the devil. Here he comes." I said, just as Korhn dropped right in front of the princess.

She gasped. Korhn had an apple in his paw.

"Is that all you could find?" I asked him. He started to argue, when Sophia interrupted.

"No, that will be fine, I'll-" She started to say as she was getting up. Then she noticed her right leg.

"Aah!!" She cried out and fell back down. "Ah! What happened to my leg?"

"It's broken." I explained. "It got crushed under the carriage we were on. Luckily, you yourself didn't get crushed."

She observed her leg. It was wrapped in bandages as well and had a primitive splint on it to make sure the bone stayed in place. It had been bleeding a bit, but I stopped it with the bandages. She wouldn't be able to walk for a while, though.

"Hey, Korhn." I called him. His head shot around to look at me. I pointed to Princess Sophia. "Give her the apple."

Korhn nodded and immediately ran up to hand the apple to Sophia. "Why, thank you." She smiled at my raccoon. "You know, you are adorable."

I chuckled. "Not all the time. He's fierce in battle. Did you see him attack those soldiers?"

I rubbed Korhn's head. "You were fantastic, my friend."

He chattered happily. Princess Sophia gazed at Korhn. Then she turned her gaze to me.

I looked at her. "What?"

"Do you really think he understands what you're saying?" She questioned me.

I scoffed. "Did you not just see me tell him to give you the apple?"

She gave me a suspicious smile. "You may have taught him a few tricks, but you can't actually talk to him."

"Really?" I asked her. "Okay, give me something to tell him."

Sophia seemed a bit surprised at that. She started to think.

Then she smiled evilly. "Okay. Tell him to hang from a tree by his tail."

I shook my head. "Raccoons aren't monkeys. Their tails don't work that way. Even if I told him to do that, he wouldn't be able to."

Princess Sophia scoffed. "Fine...then have him hang from his paws."

I sighed with a smile. "You really want me to tell him to do that?"

She nodded. "But I bet you can't."

I sighed and turned to Korhn. "Korhn, she wants you to hang from a tree by your paws."

Korhn screeched angrily at me. I just threw up my hands.

"It's what she asked. She thinks you don't understand me."

Korhn looked over at Princess Sophia with an offended look. She giggled at the look he gave her.

Korhn hesitated, but then ran up a tree and carefully gripped a branch. Then, ever so cautiously, he slowly lowered himself until he was hanging from the tree. His back legs were kicking furiously the entire time. No doubt he was scared of falling.

Sophia started laughing. "My goodness! How did you get him to do that?"

"Simple." I responded. "I just asked him to."

Then I motioned Korhn to get down before he fell.

Too late. Korhn's paws slipped and fell to the ground below him.

Sophia gasped at that. "Oh, you poor dear!"

She held out her arms, not being able to get up because of her leg. Korhn waddled over into her arms and she stroked him gently.

"So, now do you believe me?" I asked her as Korhn let out a pleasant mutter.

She laughed. "More than I did, but I'm not completely convinced."

Then all of a sudden, the princess seemed to become discouraged.

"What's wrong?" I asked her.

"Nathan, where are we?" She asked, hanging her head. "We're in this forest, both hurt, in an enemy Nation and constantly being hunted. I can't walk, you're completely worn out from saving me, and we've been separated from my parents and Jonathan."

"Oh, thank goodness we got separated from them." I thought silently.

"Not to mention, do you even know your way around Mirrac?" She glanced up at me with sad eyes. "I don't know you, but I don't believe that you've spent much time here."

I sighed. "You'd be surprised where I've been."

She gave a puzzled look. "Really? Where?"

I hesitated. This was a dangerous road to go down. I didn't know this girl too well. She was my ticket out of death by King William's hand. That was it, nothing more. I didn't exactly want to spill a bunch of personal stories to her. If I told her that I had traveled everywhere, she might wonder why.

"*No.*" I told myself. "*I won't tell her that. But…I can tell her where I've been. Yeah, that's okay to say, but that's* **all** *I'm telling her.*"

I sat there a bit, trying to find the right words so she wouldn't become curious.

"I…I've been almost everywhere." I told her as I looked up at the sky. The sun was nearly below the horizon. "I got around a lot. Once a thief is known, he has to disappear."

"Have you been here in Mirrac?" Sophia questioned.

I nodded, watching the sun disappear and night fall around us. "Many times. I've been here the most."
Sophia gave me another suspicious smile. "But I thought you said that once a thief is known, he has to disappear. Why would you come back here, Nathan?"

"*Ceruxda.*" I muttered under my breath.

"What was that?" Princess Sophia asked me.
"Nothing." I told her. "I was just…looking for someone…"
"Who were you looking for?" She pressed me.
"*Well, that plan worked fabulously.*" I thought sarcastically. "*Just don't tell her who you're looking for.*"
"I was looking for Leos." I said.
"*Why did you just tell her that?!*" My logic screamed at me.
"Who?" Sophia asked.
"Eh, Leos." I cleared my throat. "The bald guy with the battle axe that broke into your room."
Her face became concerned and confused. "Him? Seth's assassin? Why would you go after him? Wait, you know him?"
I nodded. "Yes. I know him from a long time ago."
"Was he a friend?"
"Nearly family."
"But he wanted to kill you!" She was in shock. "He was going to cut you in two! Why would he do that?! What in the world happened?!"

I wanted the questions to end there. I didn't want to answer her again, but I also knew she would keep asking until I gave her something.
So I gave her something.
I pushed my cloak behind my back and began to lift up my tunic under it, but I left my mask and cloak on. The princess became quiet and gave a look of perplexity. She began to blush as I showed my bare chest. Upon it, my massive scar.
Sophia gasped, putting her hands over her mouth. "Leos did that to you?"
I nodded grimly. "He did."
"Why?" She asked me. "How did you even survive that?"
I observed the pale reminder of my failure to defeat Leos.

"I was saved by a friend of mine." I explained as I put my tunic and cloak back on.

"This man was like family to you and yet he attacked you?" The princess marveled.

I could feel a tear coming.

"*No!*" I thought angrily. I wiped it away as soon as it came. "*No more crying!*"

"Can we stop talking about this?" I asked her, though it was never a question. "The point is, I know my way around Mirrac. We've been heading southwest and we need to continue heading in that direction."

Princess Sophia stayed quiet for a moment.

Then she mentioned, quietly. "More west then south. If we go too south, we'll end up in Hertue or Gronk."

I recalled a mental image of a map of Dedonaarc in my head. I wasn't quite sure how south or how west we should have traveled.

I turned back to the Princess. "Do you have a map of Dedonaarc?"

She shook her head. "No, but perhaps there's one in that carriage we stole."

I dismissed the idea. "No, we can't go back there."

Princess Sophia seemed puzzled. "Why not?"

I listed the reasons. "Well, the Mirracians probably already found it, I can't carry you in the condition I'm in, and I'm not leaving you here alone and defenseless."

"I'll have Korhn." She reasoned. "You said yourself that he was fierce."

"It's not just soldiers I'm worried about, though they would probably get through Korhn easily." I told her. Korhn screeched at me. I ignored him "It's also wild animals. What if a bear comes, or some big cat? Korhn wouldn't stand a chance against either of those."

"We need it. You need to go." The princess suddenly ordered me. "Go and get that map. I order you to."

I scoffed. "Sorry, your highness, but I don't take orders from you. I'm simply getting you home. That's it."

Princess Sophia seemed to grow angry as I sat below a tree and tried to take a quick nap.

"You *do* have to obey me!" She growled. "I am your princess!"

I laughed. "*My* princess? Lady, you don't even know where I'm really from. I could be from Hertue for all you know."

That comment suddenly made all of Princess Sophia's anger vanish. "Are you? Is that why you won't take off your veil?"

"Veil?" I sat up and looked at her. I pointed to my mask. "I don't wear veils. *This* is a mask."

"Well, that answers the question of whether or not you're Hertuen." Sophia said with an annoyed tone. "And what does it matter whether it's a veil or a mask? They're basically the same thing."

"Masks are manlier." I told her, folding my arms.

"Tell that to a Hertuen man." Sophia scoffed. "I'm sure he'd love to hear that."

"Why do you want to see my face anyway?" I asked her randomly. That caught her off guard. She got a nervous look.

"I-I don't." She stammered, looking away from me.

"Right." I said sarcastically. "Anyway, I'm not getting up until tomorrow morning. If you really want, *you* go get that map."

Her anger returned. "Nathan! Go and get that map now!"

"And why should I?" I asked, shutting my eyes. "We don't even know if there is one."

Princess Sophia groaned in frustration and then went silent.

"Finally!" I thought to myself as I began to drift off to sleep.

Suddenly, I heard a scraping sound. I lifted my head up to find Princess Sophia using my knife to carve a log that had been lying next to her.

"What are you doing with my knife?" I groaned.

"This is not your knife!" She lifted it up so I could see it. "This is Jonathan's! You stole it!"

"Fine." I conceded. "What are you doing with the knife I stole?"

"I'm making a walking stick for myself so I can go and get that map." She said firmly. "I'm doing what you said. *I'm* going to go get it. You can just sit here on your lazy butt while I go."

I sighed and threw back my head. "Oh, *yrojuhí adérae scytuuxby-*

bojrano!"

Sophia stopped and looked up at me. "What did you say?"

"Nothing." I grunted.

"It's not nothing." Sophia told me. "That's twice you've spoken in a language that I can't understand. I know all of the tongues of the Nations of Dedonaarc. What form are you speaking?"

"Fine, I'll go get your map." I complained, trying to change the subject. I got up and began to head back the way we came.

"Answer my question first." She commanded. "What language were you speaking?"

I turned back to her. "I said it before and I will say it again: I do not have to do anything you say. I don't take orders from you."

"Then why are you going into the forest at my command?" She smirked.

I was getting annoyed and she could tell.

"Please, Nathan." She asked calmly, her smirk gone. "Please tell me."

"No." I whispered angrily. Then I snatched the emerald knife from her and went into the dark woods.

SETH

Some of my soldiers returned after nightfall, empty handed. A few didn't return at all. I never would have believed it. My men bested by a common thief. Leos opened the doors to the throne room. I was pouring my finest wine into a goblet as he approached.

"So?" I asked him. He looked nervous.

"Sir?" He asked back.

"First, how did the boy get in here? Second, how did he get through my soldiers? Thirdly, how did he escape?"

Leos swallowed. "I...brought the bandit here, sir."

"A bandit? You brought a bandit?"

"He was among the prisoners I brought from Iarrag." Leos continued.

I laughed. "And why would I ever require someone so insignificant as a pick-pocket?"

I could hear the fear in Leos' voice. "He...was a...Hieun, sir."

I froze and my hand released the pitcher of wine. It shattered when it hit the tiled floor. Wine spilled over the floor.

"Are you certain?" I whispered as my gaze met Leos'.

He nodded.

"A Hieun?" I gasped. "Who?"

"He is called Iveslo. In the common tongue, it translates into 'Nathan'." Leos said quietly.

I glared at him. "Nathan? That is Benjamin's son, yes?"

Leos was sweating. "Yes."

"So I was not mistaken." I said quietly. "That boy *did* have silver eyes...And why is he not dead?"

Leos remained speechless.

"Speak!" I shouted at him. "How did the son of the Eirgan live?! You told me they were all dead!"

Leos shuddered as I raged. "My lord, I hacked his chest open and left him there, dying. I assumed he was dead."

I began to calm down. "Do you know what this means?"

Leos nodded.

I put my hand to my face. "This changes much. Jacob will not like this."

"I will kill him, my lord." Leos affirmed.

I sighed as I gazed back at him. "Then do it."

He began to leave.

"Leos." I called to him.

He turned around to me. "Sir?"

"Do ensure there are not others. There was a reason I had you kill them all."

"Yes, my lord." He said. Leos then bowed and left the room.

I put my hand to my forehead again. Carlisle nudged my arm, attempting to console me. I stroked his head.

"A Hieun criminal, rescuing the royal family of Ferandar." I mused aloud. "Truly, he has blurred the line between heroes and thieves. Most fascinating."

Carlisle moaned softly as I continued to stroke his fur.

"This does change much, my old friend." I spoke to him.

Nathan…

A good name.

A strong name.

"However…It may be for the better." I whispered.

I began to smile.

NATHAN

I grumbled as I trodded through the forest. I was tripping over almost everything.

"Yeesh, I'm so tired." I complained. "Stubborn princess. Why didn't I just send Korhn to do this?"

It was pitch black underneath the shade of the trees. Luckily, there was a full moon out, so once I got from underneath the trees, I could see more clearly. As I walked, I tried to keep my ears open, listening for any remains of patrolling soldiers. Just as a precaution, I had my knife drawn.

Sorry, Jon's knife.

I began observing it in the moonlight. The emeralds on the handle and sheath gleamed beautifully with the light of the moon.

"Wow." I gasped in awe. "I don't care whose knife this is. I'm keeping it."

I stopped for a moment to take another look around. It was hard to remember where the carriage was because of how quickly we had to get away from it. I had remembered that there was a whole bunch of undergrowth we had to move through when fleeing the Mirracians. I distinctly recalled that because of how many times Jon tripped over in it.

I couldn't help but chuckle at the memory. I began searching for a large area of bushes and shrubbery. Sure enough, I found the right direction before long. As I moved through it, I could easily understand why Jon would have trouble running through it. Feet could get snatched up without any difficulty. Even mine were.

"This seemed easier when I was running for my life." I muttered. Then I laughed to myself. "I suppose I could just find a dangerous animal to run from."

Then I glanced up at the tree branches above me.

I scratched my chin. "Or I could just run along the branches."

I had traveled along tree branches before in Mirrac. Mirracian trees were known for their height and density. Very firm, dizzingly tall, and dependably strong. Built to last through the strong storms of Mirrac. Their branches were likewise broad and sturdy. Able to hold my weight easily, as long as I stepped on the right branches. Traveling through the trees wouldn't be much faster than walking on the ground, but I would get a better view and stay more concealed. The more I thought about it, the more I considered how much I needed to keep some kind of stealth. Up to that point, I had simply been angrily marching through the forest. Even Mirracian guards would have been able to spot that. It was only a miracle they had not found me already. With that, I decided to take the high road. I was still extremely tired, however, and didn't feel like climbing a tree. Too much effort for my current state.

I noticed, however, a large boulder lied a few yards ahead of me. A strong branch was hanging not too high above it. I calculated that, if I got a running start, I could leap off of the boulder and catch the branch. Hardly any climbing necessary.

I backed up some, getting a good distance away. I took off for the boulder, mentally picturing how I would plant my foot on the top of the boulder and bound off of it and snatch the branch with my hands. Very simple, but I did need to make sure I got my footing right. As I neared the boulder, I kept my eyes fixed on it, making sure I was focused on where my foot was going.

But as I came within a few feet of the boulder, I saw something yellow on it.

Two small glowing spots of yellow.

Bugs?

They were little slits…just like…

Eyes.

Staring right at me.

That boulder wasn't a boulder.

I frantically tried to stop my feet as the creature arose out of its camouflage. It swung a massive, clawed arm at me. I jumped to the left to evade it. I rolled into a tree and desperately tried to get up as I turned to see the creature.

It stood in the moonlight, about ten feet away from me. It's piercing yellow eyes were fixed on mine. As it gazed at me, it let out a low hum.

I began sweating. This seemed to entertain the creature. It knew I was terrified. It bared its teeth, showing me how large its fangs were. They were a little smaller than my hand, which is huge when it comes to teeth.

I gulped. I had heard rumors of this monster. And the rumors were true. The Mirracian Conguar. A huge, dark grey creature. The size of the beast was around my height. The shape of its body was almost like an ape: it had small short legs and massive arms. It used its arms to walk, on its knuckles. Other than that, it was drastically different. It had three enormous claws at the end of its arms. Its face was like that of a Dragon, except its snout was extremely short. It had several horns on its crown and slit eyes that seemed to glare right through me. Its mouth had two massive fangs and several smaller, razor sharp teeth. It was said that the Conguar was an opportunist when it came to feeding. I now knew why. I had never heard of such amazing camouflage. Had it not been for its eyes, I would have been killed and eaten before I ever knew it was anything but a rock.

But as I stood there, watching it, I began to think that this animal was not a predator that hunted.

More like a predator that waited for the prey to come to it.

Hence the boulder camouflage.

That gave me a chance. Waiting predators weren't exactly very fast, in my experience. It was probably why it had not advanced at me yet.

But it still looked tremendously hungry.

"So, you're the Conguar, eh?" I spoke nervously.

It tilted its head to the side. I knew that it couldn't understand me. Only raccoons could understand me.

"Well, are you going to eat me or not?" I tried to sound tough.

The Conguar seemed offended at my tone. It hummed again, which was probably its growl.

"Bring it on." I challenged.

That got to it. It lifted its tree-trunk size arm to slash at me.

It *was* slow! I was right!

I dove to the side as it slashed deep into the tree that I was standing in front of. I sprinted off, having no idea where I was headed. I just knew I had to put as much distance between me and that monster as I could. But it was faster than I assumed. It may have been slow to slash at me, but it was gaining on me as we ran. It sounded similar to an elephant, crashing through the forest on a rampage.

I kept running, jumping over logs, trying my best to lose it. It was no use. The Conguar was stuck on my trail and getting very close. Another factor: I was still exhausted.

I jumped over another log and glanced back for one instant. The Conguar seemed to be losing speed. I felt a rush of relief. It could rush at rapid speeds within short distances, not long ones.

However, when I looked back again, I shrieked like a little girl. The Conguar, seeing that it was losing me, had picked up a decent sized rock and chucked it right at me.

I dropped to the ground as the rock flew over me. This caught the Conguar off guard. It actually ran right past me, unable to stop so quickly. It was still running, but was trying to skid to a halt. It stumbled, tried to regain its footing, and finally crashed into a dead tree. When the creature hit the tree, the tree's rotting foundations gave way. What was left of the tree collapsed on top of the Conguar.

I took that to my advantage and scurried up another tree. As soon as I was out of sight, the Conguar ripped the tree apart. It glanced around for me, but I made sure I wasn't seen and that I made no sound.

I even held my breath.

Then both I and the Conguar snapped our heads to look left of us when we heard rustling in the bushes.

A plump Mirracian guard peeked through the bushes.

"Oh no!" He screamed and turned to run. The Conguar chased after him and was right on his heels. After a couple of minutes, I heard several screams. More than one person. I assumed that the fat soldier ran back to his camp and now the Conguar had a bountiful feast.

I began breathing again. I glanced around where I was.

Then I noticed: I was back where the carriage crashed. I spotted the wreck a little ways below the sharp turn. The soldiers must have been waiting to ambush us if we came back.

Huh.

Once I was sure it was safe, I crawled down from the tree I had hidden in and cautiously made my way to the carriage. I searched through it and, sure enough, found a map of Dedonaarc:

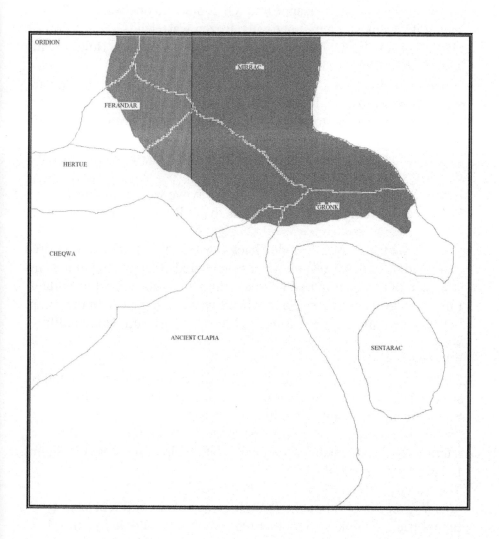

ORIDION

MIRRAC

FERANDAR

HERTUE

GRONK

CHEQWA

ANCIENT CLAPIA

SENTARAC

Unfortunately, it didn't show any cities. I soon discovered that the dark outline was showing what areas were under Mirracian control. Only Cheqwa, the desert Nation, and Sentarac, the island Nation of the banished, were untouched. Clapia was open to anyone, seeing that the Clapians had long ago disappeared. Of course, no one wanted Clapia, seeing it was mostly a mountainous, frozen wasteland.

"Well." I said aloud. "Mirrac isn't fighting just Ferandar. Bold. I really hope Seth has bitten off more than he can chew."

I focused, getting back on track. Lord Seth's palace was in the upper right corner of Mirrac. It was there for two reasons:

1. If someone wanted to attack it, they'd have to go through nearly all of Mirrac to get there.

2. It was a very nice place there. It was near the coast and had beautiful weather.

It was then that I realized just how far away we were from Iarrag.

We had a very long way to go if I was to get Princess Sophia home.

I took the map and headed back towards my camp. I was so tired that I had to stop and rest numerous times. I also felt sharp pains in my stomach, but I was too tired to do anything or to consider it important. I began to grow extremely faint when I was coming close to the camp, but I blamed my fatigue. Strangely, I felt dizzy as well. Unnaturally weak.

"*Bad fish.*" I reasoned.

Still, something was nagging at me. I kept feeling like I was forgetting something. There was another reason that I was feeling like this.

Suddenly, a sharp pain ached in my stomach.

"Aah!" I groaned in pain. The ache made me lurch forward. I threw my hands over my stomach, hoping that would help in some way. It didn't. I was breathing heavily.

Too heavily.

"*Really bad fish?*" I thought, though I was not as confident as last time. I tried to think of any other reason why I would be like this, but my brain was just too worn out to think that hard. I kept moving forward. I glanced at my arm and noticed something on the sleeve of my cloak. It was wet.

"*Did it rain?*" I wondered, looking up. No sign of clouds. "*Could I have missed that?*"

I assumed that I had, knowing how exhausted I was. I kept walking, trying to move on despite the sharp pains in my stomach. When I got back to the camp, I knew that it was only a couple of hours before the sun rose. Princess Sophia was asleep.

I envied her sleep. That, in turn, led to anger.

"Princess, wake up!" I shouted.

She snapped up, swinging some sort of rock around.

"What?! What is it?!" She screamed, looking everywhere around her. I threw the map at her face. The map surprised her and she swung her rock at it.

"Here's your stinking map!" I snarled fiercely. I was cranky.

She glared at me. "Well, no need to be like that! Treat me with a little respect, why don't you? Ugh, why is this map wet?"

"It rained." I growled, about to just lie down and fall asleep. "Deal with it, your majesty."

I fell over, not purposely. My feeling of weakness was growing rapidly. *"Am I this tired?"* I pondered, but really didn't care.

"Nathan?" Sophia's voice rang out, but it sounded far away. "It didn't rain…"

Her voice suddenly became so hushed that I couldn't hear her anymore.

"What did you say?" I mumbled, feeling something wet under me.

Unexpectedly, I felt Princess Sophia's hands on me. She flipped me over onto my back.

"What?!" I raged at her, but I saw genuine fear in her eyes. Her mouth moved, but I couldn't hear anything. She put her hand to my forehead.

"What are you doing?" I questioned. "I'm not sick, I'm just tired."

But then…I saw something on her hands…

Blood.

"Blood?" I thought. *"Is she bleeding? Is that why she's scared?"*

Then I glanced down at my stomach. My stomach that was having sharp pains. My stomach that I had bandaged because…

Because…

"Why is it so hard to think?!" I raged in my mind. *"Why did I bandage it?!"*

The princess got up and grabbed my arm. She began pulling and dragging me across the dirt.

Then I remembered. I had been wounded. Had my wound opened up again? Had I lost a lot of blood?

It would explain a lot.

"I'm hurt." I managed to get out. Now it was difficult just to speak. I could feel my body shutting down. Sophia put her hand on my cheek and brought her face close to mine. She was yelling by the look of her, but I couldn't hear anything.

I read her lips and made out what she was saying.

"Stay with me!"

I don't remember much after that.

I began to hear again. It felt like I had been trapped in some horrible void between reality and sleep for hours. Thankfully, it ended and my vision was beginning to return, too.

"Is he going to be all right?" I heard, faintly.

It was Princess Sophia.

"Quiet, girl." A rough voice replied to her.

"Girl?" I thought. *"She's the princess. Does he know who he's talking to? And she said I needed to show respect."*

I just sat wherever I was for what felt like another hour. There were times when I finally fell asleep and escaped the torture of pain that I had running through me. However, most of the dreams I had were nightmares. If not from my past, they were of the present. Sleep became just as horrible as being awake. Eternities past. It felt like forever…Until…

"Nathan, honey?" I heard clearly.

I opened my eyes. My vision was a bit blurry, but I could tell that the princess was on my right. She was very close to me. It was like we were cuddling. The position made me uncomfortable, so I tried to shove her away. Unfortunately, I was still too weak to do much. She simply took my shove and wasn't pushed back the slightest.

Sophia got closer and tried to whisper something in my ear, but I sat upright and tried to get away from her.

"Dearest, settle down." She told me, nervously.

"Dearest?" I questioned groggily. "What are you talking about?"

Then, my vision came back fully. I was in a small room. Though it was a small room, there were many medical supplies around. There were also three others in the room: Princess Sophia, Korhn, and an elderly man. Korhn was in Sophia's arms. I took a closer look at Sophia and noticed that she was no longer in the beautiful dress.

She was in peasant garments. I was awestruck by this.

"That doesn't look right." I never thought the daughter of such a prideful man could ever know such humility. She also had a walking stick and was using it to lean on instead of her broken leg.

I then noticed that she was trying to signal me with a look. She seemed to be very nervous and she nodded her head towards the elderly man ever so subtly. My gaze turned to the elderly man. He was washing his hands in a basin. I assumed, considering the medical supplies and the fact that my wounds had been treated, that he was a physician.

A Mirracian physician.

That was it. When I began to fade away, Sophia must have panicked and brought me to a physician nearby. Of course, she couldn't go to him looking like she did. He would have known right away that she was royalty and Lord Seth had no daughter. But what story did she create?

"'Honey'. 'Dearest'." I noted. *"She must have told him I'm her husband."*

I groaned at the thought, but it was a good idea. Couples in Mirrac married at young ages. Lovers often got impatient here, it seemed.

"How are you feeling, Nathan?" The princess asked me, putting her hand on my shoulder. She was trying to play the part of a worried wife and not doing a bad job.

I'd just have to play the part of a reassuring husband.

Great.

"I'm fine." I told her as lovingly as I could.

The physician suddenly approached me with a cup filled with water. "You've lost a lot of blood." He told me with the rough voice I had heard earlier. "You'll need to drink plenty of fluids. Eating would be a good idea too. It'll be some time before you recover your full strength."

I gratefully took the cup and began drinking. After I finished, I handed the cup back to the physician. He went to refill it.

"What happened?" I coughed. I needed to know what the princess had told this physician.

"Your wife tells me you were attacked by some beast." The physician said, returning with more water. "It's a good thing she got you here in time. You are very fortunate to have her."

Now was the time to sell the idea that I had a dear wife whom I cherished.

"Yes." I smiled under my mask. I cautiously got off the table and embraced Sophia tightly. I could tell that she was barely able to bear my filthiness. She was holding her breath.

"Thank you, Sophia." I said kindly.

"I was so worried about you." She added in. "It was so frightening seeing you like that. I'm just so happy that you're all right."

She mustered up her strength and hugged me closely. This was one brave princess. I mean, she knew I walked through sewers.

I caught eye of the physician. He had a big smile on his face.

"Oh, no you don't." He chuckled, pointing a finger at me. "You don't get off that easy. She just saved you. Don't you think she deserves an 'I love you'?"

I was glad I was wearing a mask right then, because I gave a worried look.

"Tell her I love her?" I thought. *"That's just spectacular."*

But I looked down at Sophia and in the most affectionate and tender voice I had, I said to her:

"I love you, Sophia."

For a moment, Sophia's eyes blinked with a strange emotion hiding in them. Part of that was an aura of discomfort. That made sense. We hardly knew each other and I was telling her 'I love you'. But there was another part. An emotion that…I was not so sure of its origins. But it was only there for an instant. Then it was gone.

She replied with the same tone. "And I love you, Nathan."

"Three days." I thought to myself. *"We've known each other for three days and we're acting like a married couple. If Nila was here, she would be laughing."*

Sophia turned to the physician. "How can I repay you for saving my love?"

I shuddered at that. We had absolutely **nothing** to offer.

Thankfully, the physician simply shook his head.

"No charge. I'm just happy to see you two back together." Then something sparked in the elderly man's eyes. "Hey! Why don't you both spend the night?"

No way was I keeping up that act for an entire night.

"Actually we really should be going." I told him firmly. "We need to get home."

Sophia winced. The physician gave a puzzled look.

"But your wife said you were a long ways from your home." He told me.

I groaned. Sophia hit me, playfully.

"Oh, honey! You forget everything!" She laughed.

I played along. "Oh, yes! Of course! How foolish of me! Yes, we are a far ways from home, but we don't want to burden you."

"Actually, I would like to stay for a litt-" Sophia began.

"Hush, dear." I told her.

"Oh, no. Please stay just this night." The physician insisted. "Really, I wouldn't want you to be out there. After all, you're in no shape to travel right now. After some food and rest, you can be on your way. Plus, there are rumors of a Conguar roaming these parts."

My eyes widened. The Conguar.

"Well, it is late." I said quickly. "Thank you for your hospitality."

"Okay, what did you tell him?" I asked Sophia as I sipped on more of my water.

The physician had given us a small meal of bread and pears. We had eaten quickly, claiming we were ready to go to bed so we could start traveling early. The physician had left us in a spare bedroom.

Sophia was sitting on the bed. "I simply told him that we were traveling, newly married, and that you were attacked by an animal."

"What about my clothes? Does he think I'm a thief?" I pressed her.

She shook her head. "I told him you were a Hertuen and that you were wearing some traditional clothing that you hardly removed. That explains both the smell and the veil."

"Mask." I corrected her.

Sophia rolled her eyes. "Whatever."

I observed her staff.

"Where'd you get that?" I pointed.

"Same place I got these." Sophia gestured to her clothes. "I traded my dress to a poor widow woman. You should have seen how happy she was. She added in the staff. She was a kind lady."

I noted that the garments were a bit too big on her.

"And your leg?" I asked.

"I told the physician the truth." She explained. "We were traveling in a wagon and it fell over a hill. I was hurt in the process."

I sighed with relief. She had thought through a lot of this. She was smart.

"Good." I said, feeling a bit less uneasy. "Very good. Well…I suppose the next thing for us is to get some rest. We both need it."

"Agreed." Sophia nodded.

And with that, we both began preparing to go to sleep. I was still fairly tired and Sophia had dragged me to a nearby village and acted as the worried wife all day. We didn't speak much until we were both ready for sleep. I gave Sophia the bed while I took the floor.

But, of course, I found myself unable to sleep. I was worried that we hadn't played the part well enough and that the physician was going to get a bunch of soldiers to come and take us in the night.

I found out that Sophia wasn't able to sleep either.

"Nathan?" She whispered. "Are you awake?"

"Yes, I'm awake." I whispered back.

"I can't sleep." She told me.

"Why not?"

"I'm scared."

I sat up a bit and glanced at her up in the bed. "You're scared?"

She looked down at me and nodded. "I'm worried that the Mirracians will discover who we are."

I lied back down. "Me too."

"*You're* scared?" Sophia asked, sounding surprised.

"Yes, I am." I told her. "Did you think that thieves don't get scared? We get scared all the time. Just think what happens when we get caught. It's terrifying."

Sophia remained silent for a while. Then she spoke. "What's it like?"

"Getting caught?"

"No, having to steal." Sophia clarified. "Do you feel guilty when you do it? Do you get a thrill from it?"

I thought about the questions she asked me. "Well…I didn't like to steal when I started out, but now I do. There *is* a thrill from it. I don't really think of what it's doing to the person because then I do feel guilty."

"Would you like to have the choice not to steal?" Sophia asked softly.

I paused. It sounded like she was offering me something. The chance to live at the castle. Maybe as a worker or a servant.

"Why do you ask?" I asked suspiciously.

"I'm curious." She confessed.

"Are you offering me that chance?"

Sophia was silent for a long time. "Do you *want* that chance?"

I thought about it. "I…I don't know. It sounds nice, I guess."

"Were you always a thief?"

"No."

"What were you?"

"Just a normal kid." I explained.

"Were you the son of a blacksmith?"

I was puzzled that she suggested that. "No, what made you think that?"

"When you and Jonathan fought, you drove your shoulder into a weak point of his armor." She told me. "A blacksmith would've known where those weak points were located. You did that intentionally, didn't you?"

That had all been by chance. I had no idea where the weak points of Jon's armor were.

"Well, no." I said. "I was the son of a warrior. He taught me everything I know."

"What happened to him?"

"I already told you before." I said. "My parents are dead."

"Were they killed by Leos?" Sophia asked curiously.

"…Yes."

"That's why you were searching for him, isn't it?"

"Yeah."

"You're scared of him." She said plainly. "I saw the way you ran when you first saw him. I was scared of him too, but you seemed terrified."

"You don't know what he's like."

"What *is* he like?"

"He killed many other families, besides my own. He's very good at what he does." I told her.

"But you escaped." She said. "And now you want to go after him? To kill him?"

"I want to avenge my parents." I said.

"Nathan, revenge is not the way." She leaned over the bed to look at me. Her beautiful blue eyes seemed to gleam in the darkness. "Don't go after him in anger and rage. It eats you from the inside."

"How would you know?" I asked rudely. "You've never seen anything like I've seen. I've been through tragedies and what have you been through? 'Oh, dear! My servant is sick and I have to get the crumpets myself!' You live in a castle. You're a princess. You've never been through any hardship."

Sophia was still looking at me. Her eyes drooped with sorrow. "Perhaps not like yours."

I scoffed as I turned over, not wanting to face her anymore. I knew I was right. We both knew I was right.

"My father has, though." Sophia continued.

I rolled back to face her. "What are you talking about?"

She looked at me with the same sad eyes. "My father's family was killed when he was a child as well. He was the youngest out of five boys. To get to the throne, my great aunt killed my grandfather and killed all of my uncles. My father barely escaped. His nurse took him and fled the country. My father grew up as an archer for the Oridionite army and didn't return to Ferandar until he was twenty-eight. He then had to kill his own aunt and he reclaimed the throne."

I took this in. I had never before heard this story of King William. Sophia went on.

"That's the reason he hates criminals. He doesn't trust them and he thinks if he lets one get away, they'll come back and possibly kill everyone he loves. He wants me and my mother protected. That's why he hates you."

I remained silent as I thought about all of this. After a couple minutes, I spoke.

"I bet he's scared to death that you're with me."

Sophia nodded. "Yes, he probably is."

I wanted to ask her something. "Do…Do you think he'll keep his promise of pardoning me?"

Sophia's answer was without hesitation. "Of course he will. As long as you do as he asked."

We did fall asleep eventually. Exhaustion finally took over me instead of my fear of being found. But it wasn't long before I awoke. In my profession, heavy sleeping could be more of a curse than a blessing. I sat upright with a start.

"Where am I?!" My mind raced. It wasn't until I recalled the event with the physician that I calmed down. Sophia was still lying asleep in the bed above me and I didn't want to wake her. I got up and walked to the window, curious of what time it was.

It was twilight. The sun had nearly disappeared below the horizon. I was surprised that we had slept through the whole day.

I was also surprised that the physician had not found us out. Korhn hopped up on my shoulder. He gave a small chitter.

"Yeah, we should leave as soon as possible." I agreed. "The longer we're here, the more we're in danger and the higher the risk of the Mirracians catching us."

I turned back to see Sophia quietly sleeping. She was curled up in a blanket, smiling pleasantly. Most likely, she was in a happy dream world. I grew a little envious.

"Enjoy your sweet dreams while you can, Princess." I whispered. "You may not have them for much longer."

I trodded over to my bed on the floor and was planning to go back to sleep, when I heard faint noises of footsteps. I instinctively crouched low, hearing the sound that made my adrenaline rush. It was the sound someone made when trying to sneak up on someone else.

I was a professional at sneaking. I knew the sound very well. I went to the side of Sophia's bed and slowly put my hand over her mouth. Feeling my hand (and possibly smelling it), Sophia immediately awoke. She cried out, but my hand muffled her scream. I put my other hand in front of my mask and made a "Shh!" gesture. The princess panicked a bit more, but realizing what I was doing, she calmed down rather quickly. I slowly took my hand off of her mouth.

"Why must you do that?!" She whispered angrily. "You scared me half to death!"

"We have to go now." I told her, ignoring her outbursts.

"Why? What's wrong?" She questioned fearfully.

"I think we've been found out." I explained.

"How do you know?" She asked me as I crept towards the window. I peeked out, not seeing any evidence of any soldiers.

But I wasn't afraid of soldiers.

I was afraid of Leos.

"I heard them." I replied as I kept gazing out the window. "Footsteps. Sneaking footsteps."

The princess scoffed. "Sneaking footsteps? Really? Nathan, I do think you are too paranoid."

"Maybe that's why I've lived this long." I muttered under my breath.

At that moment, heavy, loud footsteps came running up the stairs to the room we were in. Sophia instantly became frightened, grabbing her staff. I unsheathed my knife, making my way to the door.

Sure enough, Mirracian soldiers burst through it. I kicked the first one and he fell into the others behind him, knocking them all back down the stairs.

"Run!" I yelled to Sophia.

"Where?!" She panicked. She was right. There was nowhere to run. We were on the second floor with our only escape blocked by Mirracian soldiers. I quickly glanced around.

Window.

Well, whatever works.

I grabbed Sophia, picking her up from the bed along with her walking stick. She shrieked in surprise as I lifted her up. I then ran towards the window.

"Nathan, no!" Sophia screamed when she realized what I was doing.

I crashed through the window, shattering it as we flew through it. The shattering glass immediately spread itself upon our bodies. I was cut across my arm and back. I tried to shield Sophia from getting cut, but the side of her stomach was sliced.

She cried out in pain as the broken glass scraped across her precious skin. I just gritted my teeth at the pain.

Then…falling. We were falling towards the hard ground below.

Sophia was screaming. I spun sideways so that my back was facing the earth. I was planning to take the entirety of the fall, so as to protect Sophia, but Sophia spun sideways as well.

It could have been a complete accident, but it seemed like she spun so that we would share the blow. For an instant, we just stared at each other in mid-air. Sophia's beautiful blue eyes were full of fear. I'm sure mine were too. It felt like an eternity passed as we fell. Then I saw

Sophia glance sideways at the ground that was zooming up at us. She braced herself. I closed my eyes.

"Oowuf!!" My breath was squeezed from my lungs. Sophia made a similar sound.

I couldn't breathe! I couldn't breathe! I desperately sucked at the air around me. I wheezed and gasped and Sophia did likewise. Sophia seemed like she had been hurt far more than I had. She probably had landed on her broken leg.

Other than being bruised and having the wind knocked out of us, we were fine. I recovered quickly and started to get up. Korhn followed us out the window. I caught him as Sophia struggled to get up, wincing sharply when she put pressure on her right leg. She began to fall back, but I held her up with my free arm.

"They went through the window!" A soldier yelled from our room at the top of the physician's house. I tossed Korhn into Sophia's arms.

"Hold onto him!" I told her as I lifted her up.

Then I saw him come from behind the house.

Leos.

His dark red armor was gone. In its place, he wore some older clothing that I recognized. Thin, brown, leather armor.

Hieun-made and the very same armor he wore when he slew my family.

Leos immediately charged at me, holding his axe high. He was too close to run from. So I improvised.

I picked Sophia up and ran at Leos with her in my arms.

"Nathan, what are you doing?!" Sophia screamed at me.

Leos just began to realize what I was planning as I approached him. We both froze with about a yard's distance between us. Leos grew furious.

We both knew he could not harm Sophia. I held her against me like a shield.

"Your move." I smiled. Sophia was silently shaking, holding both Korhn and her walking stick very closely to her chest.

Leos was weighing his options. I could see his thoughts processing in his mind:

"*Kill them both and face Seth? Or lose them both and face Seth?*"

Leos growled and glanced behind him. He gave a whistle as he brought down his axe from its high position.

I wasn't the only one with a pet. Leos had a pet as well.

It stomped from behind the house. An elephant. His name was Saums.

"You know you can't win this." Leos gestured toward Saums. "You remember last time you saw him?"

"I remember that I killed one of those things." I replied.

Leos furrowed his brow. He gave a small grunt. "Fine. Give me the girl and I'll let you go free."

Sophia gulped. I laughed.

"You're lying." I told him. "You want me dead. You'd never let me go away freely if you had the chance to take me out."

Leos grew a bit angrier. I had seen right through his bluff.

"Fine, I am lying. Just drop the princess and face me like a man." He challenged.

"I won't survive." I replied plainly. "And you won't play fair."

"Your father knew both of those things, yet he fought." Leos smiled.

"I'm not my father." I responded with a snarl.

"Of course you're not." Leos laughed. "The Eirgan would never have stooped so low to the degree of a thief."

"Or the degree of a murderer." I countered.

That got him mad again. "Give me the girl, Iveslo!"

"Why don't you take her from me, Shiako?!" I roared back.

Neither of us moved. I needed a distraction, but I had none. Leos was deadly just by himself. With Saums at his back, even if I was using the princess as a shield, we weren't going to last long. I had only managed this much time because Leos believed I would actually put Sophia in harm's way. I desperately tried to think of something, anything I could do.

I came up with nothing.

"Sir!" Mirracian guards started running out of the physician's house. Leos kept his eyes fixed on me. Suddenly, the most delightful thing happened. The guard was about to say more, but it seemed that one guard tripped over the door's threshold, knocking into all of the other guards. They all tumbled over like infants trying to walk for the first time. Leos couldn't help but move his gaze to stare at the pathetic men he had with him.

And that was my chance.

I turned and ran. I made little noise as I bolted with Princess Sophia in my arms, so Leos didn't notice until a few good seconds had passed. He charged after me, but couldn't keep up for long. I had a head start and I was much faster than Leos. Unfortunately, Saums was chasing after me as well.

"Don't let him get away!" Leos shouted. His elephant began charging faster, releasing a deep bellow as he did.

Elephants are faster than most people think they are.

The beast was right on my heels. It was much faster than I was and it was challenging enough just carrying Sophia.

Saums was on my tail as soon as Leos ordered him to charge. I wouldn't outrun him for long, but I could probably make it to the tree line. If I made it there, I had a good chance I would lose Saums.

I glanced behind me. Saums's tusk was literally just a few feet from impaling me. I knew the elephant wouldn't, for I had Sophia with me. Saums was just trying to stop me.

I used all of my energy that I had gained from the hours of sleep and sprinted. My legs pushed furiously. So furiously, in fact, that I was staying ahead of Saums.

I was running as fast as an elephant.

I wouldn't be able to do it for very long at all, though. I was dead-tired and I was carrying both a young woman and a raccoon. This amazing speed that I had reached was a result of panic, adrenaline, and the will to live. They were not enough to keep me at this pace.

I was quickly slowing, but Saums kept constant.

"Nathan, you have to go faster!" Sophia ordered.

"I can't!" I uttered breathlessly. "I can't!"

"Please, Nathan!" Sophia begged. "Run! Run! You can do it! I believe that you can do this!"

I don't know why, but there was something inside of me that just heeded her words. Something happened because of what she said to me.

"You can do it! I believe that you can do this!"

I pushed myself to go faster. I forced my legs to go on.

And I did. I began running faster than Saums. I began to pull away from him.

Running faster than an elephant.

"That's it, Nathan!" Sophia cheered. "Keep going!"

But I could not do that forever. My lungs were burning, my legs felt like they were going to burst, my heart was beating faster than it ever had before.

The trees! They were so close! I ran at them!

"Don't quit, Nathan!" Sophia ordered. "Don't quit!

Twenty yards! Eighteen yards! Fifteen yards! I was nearly there!

Behind me, Saums noticed that I was now breaking away from him. He increased his speed.

"*NO!*" I shouted in my thoughts.

"Run, Nathan! Run as fast as you can!!" Sophia yelled.

So close!! So close!!

I dived passed the tree line. I threw Sophia so I wouldn't fall on top of her. She landed in the darkness of the trees and I landed face first into the dirt.

I could not move.

"Nathan, get up!" Sophia crawled over to me. "He's still coming!"

I didn't even respond. How could I? I was trying to recover so much air that anything else was impossible. I just lied in the darkness of the trees in the night.

With one of my ears placed in the dirt, it was easy to hear the rumbling of Saums coming extremely close. I knew Leos wasn't far behind, either.

I gave up. Korhn and I were going to be killed by Leos and Sophia would be captured to eventually see the same fate.

"I'm sorry." I whispered weakly to Sophia. That was all I could do.

Then...the rumbling stopped. Saums had stopped running.

...Sophia gasped.

I used the rest of my strength to tilt my head ever so slightly. I could see Sophia's face.

It was that of pure terror.

"*Of Leos?*" I pondered.

Then I tilted my head just enough to see where she was looking...

Where Saums was looking...

Where Leos was looking...

It was in a tree.
The Mirracian Conguar.

"*Ceruxda.*" I groaned.

The beast instantly leaped for Saums.
Maybe the Conguar thought it could eat Saums. Maybe it felt
threatened by Saums and just wanted to kill the elephant.
Either way, it was plain stupid if you ask me.
Saums knocked the Conguar out of the air, shrieking madly as he did.
When the Conguar fell to the ground, Saums roared again and began
trying to trample it. Leos joined Saums and began fighting the mighty
Conguar.
Another chance.
I was panting like a dog, but I had to keep going. I forced myself up,
crawling towards Sophia. My muscles cried out in anguish as I took
Sophia in my arms once again and threw her up on my shoulder. There
was no way I could run, but I could walk. I trudged as fast as I could
deeper into the woods as I heard Leos and Saums fighting the Conguar.
I slowly made my way past bushes, over tree roots, and under
branches. But I wasn't more than a hundred steps away when I heard
the fighting stop. I heard rustling in the woods as the Conguar fled past
us.
He had several deep cuts in him and he was limping. He rushed off
into the dark woods.
"*Oh no.*" I thought to myself.
Leos would be on us in no time. Saums wouldn't be able to move
through the forest, but Leos would have no trouble.
And I could hear him getting closer.
"Shepherd, save us." Sophia prayed.
I glanced over my shoulder. Leos ripped through a bush not too far
behind me. He spotted us.
"Give it up, Iveslo!" He growled. "What else can you do?"
That gave me an idea.
"Take a strategy out of your book." I grinned.
Leos gave a look of confusion.

"*Féraipetnodas!*" I yelled out. "*Heetlípli uxscy!*"

Korhn's ears perked up as I shouted this. And all throughout the woods we were in, there was a slight rustling. Leos, realizing what I had done, immediately bolted for me and Sophia. He was about thirty yards away and closing in fast. However, a certain chittering began to sound all around us. It was growing constantly louder and closer. Sophia looked around with perplexity. Leos was about to reach us when a raccoon dropped on his face, scratching his eyes. Leos screamed out, trying to get the raccoon off of him.

"Where did-?" Sophia was about to ask. I started my brisk pace once again. I was regaining my strength, so I began quickening to a jogging pace. All around Leos, raccoons came raining out of the trees. Dozens of them. One of the reasons I loved Mirrac so much was because it was thriving with so many raccoons.

And I could speak to all of them.

Soon enough, Leos was being swarmed by a wave of raccoons, all biting, scratching, clawing at any part they could find. To prevent him from swinging his axe, many of them grabbed onto it and pulled it away from him. I turned back once more to see Leos completely overwhelmed by my furry friends, unable to even stand. They flooded over him like water. You couldn't even see him in the mass of the raccoons.

"How in the world...?!" Sophia gawked as we fled far away from Leos.

CHAPTER SIX
DEV AND DANCING

SOPHIA

Several hours had passed. After about a mile or so, Nathan finally set me down and assured me that Leos would be very far behind us. Nathan set me next to a tree so I could lean up against it. He tended to the cuts I had gotten from crashing through the window. When he was finished, he put my arm over his shoulder, helping me to stand.

"Do you need help walking?" He asked me.

I pat my walking stick. "I should be fine. You've carried me long enough."

Nathan simply nodded at that and we continued walking. We were slow because of my leg, but Nathan wasn't too eager to speed up. I could see that he was already very worn once again.

We were both silent for a while.

"I believe you now." I told him after a while of quiet.

"What?" He asked.

"I believe that you can actually talk to raccoons." I explained. "What we just saw back there...I truly believe you."

Nathan laughed. "I should hope so. I wasn't lying."

I giggled. "I never thought you were lying. I thought you were crazy."

Nathan turned his head to look at me. "Huh. You and your parents both."

I frowned at that. "No, I'm not sure my parents really think you're crazy. They just...hate you."

I winced at that. It was true, but sometimes the truth is cruel.

"What a ray of sunshine you are." He replied sarcastically. However, he said it with a smile, so I don't believe he was offended.

The conversation ended for a bit as we trudged through the night.

"Do you know where we're going?" I asked.

"Southeast."

"You're sure?"

"Yep."

More silence. I then had the idea that Nathan wasn't too big on talking at the moment. He would answer me, but he wouldn't keep the conversation going. However, there was something that I was just dying to know.

"Why are you doing this?" I suddenly asked.
Nathan glanced my way, his silver eyes shining from under his hood.
"Why are you helping me?" I continued. "Why are you protecting me and going out of your way to make sure I'm safe?"
Nathan scoffed. "You, my princess, are my ticket to life. Why wouldn't I protect you? My life literally depends on it. I would be crazy to leave you."
"No." I told him with a smile. "You would be crazy to do what you're doing. You had many chances to turn in me and my family. You could have gained a big reward from Seth. Or you could have just abandoned us. Even now, you could just leave me and be on your merry way."
"But your father-" Nathan began.
"My father has a reputation of hunting thieves, that is true." I interrupted him, knowing what he was going to say. "But if you can get a royal family out of a heavily guarded castle, save a princess several times from danger while she has a broken leg, and escape from a Nation that's out to get you, you can get away from my father."
Nathan didn't say anything to that.
"Why did you free us in the first place?" I questioned him. "You could have just escaped. You could have saved yourself. Then you wouldn't have to negotiate with my father."
We kept walking. Nathan didn't say a word.
"Why are you doing this?" I asked him again.
"Because…it's the right thing to do." He answered after a while.
I thought about that answer.
"'It's the right thing to do'." I repeated. I let out a giggle. Nathan turned his masked face towards me.
"What?" He asked, sounding offended. I suppose he figured I was mocking him.
"You're not like any bandit I've ever seen or heard about." I smiled. "You care more about others than you do yourself. You're a very noble person."
His eyes softened. His gleaming silver eyes.

"And, I find that funny." I explained. "Ironic, I should say. Bandits aren't usually noble."

"Noble?" He laughed. "Oh no, I'm not noble."

"You're not?" I laughed back. "Nathan, do I really need to say it again? You rescued me and my parents from Seth's palace, you came and fought off soldiers after my father *left* you, you constantly protected me when you had absolutely no reason to other than the fact that my father is willing to pardon you, which I know you could avoid his forces easily."

Nathan was in deep thought as he continued to help me walk. I continued.

"Nathan, you are more noble than me, my father, and my mother combined." I complimented.

"No, I'm not." Nathan whispered.

"Yes you are." I told him. "Neither my parents nor I would *ever* go out of the way to save our enemy. Jonathan wouldn't even do that. You are the most noble person I have ever met. The noble bandit."

Nathan stopped walking. "Here's far enough."

He helped me sit me down on the soft grass right underneath a tree. I leaned up against the tree. Nathan sat down next to me.

"So why are you the noble bandit?" I asked aloud, not actually asking Nathan. "What culture would make you into that person?"

Nathan ignored me as I tried to piece the few puzzle pieces I had together.

I started making a list. "You're very noble, you're skilled with a sword, you want to avenge your family's death, you're not greedy, you think of others' safety before your own, you're mysterious, you're humble, you're kind when you want to be, you're determined, you're committed to finish a duty, you don't want people to know who you are."

I tried to think of what kind of people were like that. It constantly reminded me of Hertue. Hertuens had a tradition of wearing veils. Men and women alike. Not all Hertuens wore them, but it was a tradition within their culture. It was to bring honor to a great spiritual leader of their past, who had glimpsed the glory of the Shepherd. When seeing just a hint of the Shepherd's glory, the man's face glowed from that day. To keep people from being frightened of him, he wore a veil. That man was considered one of the greatest leaders in Hertuen history.

Thus, certain Hertuens wore veils so as to reverence him after his passing. It was done so often, in fact, it had become a custom in Hertue. Especially among the wise elders and leaders.

This, however, did not relate to Nathan in the least. He had little consideration for tradition and etiquette. Wearing a spiritual garment would not suit him. Also, Nathan spoke a different language than Hertuen.

He clearly wasn't Cheqwan. Cheqwans were strikingly unique when it came to their physique. Most were tall and very fit. Not only that, but living in desert country, their complexion was a dark tan. Above all, they belonged to a warrior-culture. Some families were honorable, some were back-stabbers, but all were raised to know battle. Some Nations referred to the Cheqwans as barbaric. Nathan was nothing like a typical Cheqwan. Physically or otherwise.

It was also clear that Nathan was not a Gronkon. Dark-skinned dwellers of the rain forests of Gronk, they were known to be very hospitable and open with people, not hiding anything.

An Oridionite? Could be. They were a melting pot of people, as were Ferandarons. Many cultures, many differences. Still, it didn't seem right. The language he spoke before was sticking out in my mind. Oridionite language was the common tongue in Oridion, Ferandar, and Mirrac. And I was taught to learn the languages of every Nation.

I must have missed one.

"What did Leos say?" I asked aloud, looking at Nathan. "You're the son of the...Eirgan?"

Nathan's eyes flashed at me, but he said nothing.

"What's an Eirgan?" I tried to push it out of him.

Nathan looked away from me, ignoring me.

"*He's not budging on that.*" I observed. "*Maybe if I can just narrow it down some.*"

"Just tell me where you were born." I said after a long silence.

Nathan glanced back at me. His eyes gave a hint that he was debating whether or not he should tell me.

He sighed. "Ferandar."

"*What?!*" I thought. "*Impossible! He has to be lying. I know all people in Ferandar.*"

But I looked into his eyes.

He wasn't lying.

He must have seen my confusion.

"You don't know everything about your Nation. Didn't your father ever tell you about the Hieun tribe?"

I went through my mind, searching for familiarity to that word.

"*Hieun tribe.*" Echoed in my mind.

Nothing.

"No, I've never heard of them. Is that where you're from?"

"No more questions." He said, looking up to the sky. "It's nearly morning. We better get going again."

I looked up, too. The dark blue sky was beginning to light with a purple color. Nathan rose and put my arm over his shoulder again to help me up.

I got my staff situated and we continued walking. Korhn hopped up on my shoulder.

I giggled. "Well, he trusts me now."

"Yeah. He definitely likes you." Nathan commented. "It's probably because you pet him so much."

I laughed.

Nathan chuckled a little as well. Then silence.

We had silence a lot of times. I guess that happens when two different worlds collide. The beggar with the spoiled. The hungry with the satisfied.

That actually reminded me of how hungry I was. I was in the woods, completely filthy, extremely famished, and parched.

"I am so hungry." I whimpered.

Nathan glanced at me. "Well, I could hunt something, but I doubt you'll want to eat it. With your issue and all."

I put my hand to my stomach. "I actually don't care what it is, as long as it will fill me and that it doesn't look like an animal."

Nathan pondered on this. He then looked as if he was about to ask me something, but hesitated.

"What?" I asked him.

"Well…" He looked like he wanted to find the right words.

"What is it?" I asked impatiently.

Nathan gave up and just asked me plainly:

"Do you mind if we rob someone?"

I winced. "Yes, I do mind. I'm a princess. Not a bandit."

I instantly shut my mouth, remembering who I was talking to. When I said the word 'bandit', I said it with some disgust.

Nathan seemed a bit offended. "Well, I *am* a bandit. I steal. I'm sorry if that makes me too vile for your company."

I felt bad that I had insulted him. "I didn't mean any offense, but you can't deny the fact that stealing is very wrong. What if someone did it to us?"

Nathan began to think. "Well, if we want to get technical, fruit comes from the land. Who is to say that they truly belong to one person? Just because someone claims a certain tree or plot of land doesn't mean it's automatically their property, right?"

"That's not true, and you know it." I stated. "People worked hard to grow that fruit. *They* planted the trees. *They* tilled the land. You know that it's stealing and you can't justify it."

Nathan gave an annoyed expression. "Look, I'm just trying to make it easier for your guilt. You don't need to make *me* feel guilty about this too."

"I don't want to steal." I told him firmly. "It is wrong."

"Fine." He threw up his arms. "*I'll* do the stealing. But you have to come with me. I can't leave you here alone."

"Quite the gentleman for a thief." I said a little harshly

"Oh, and maybe I could start calling you 'William'." Nathan growled back.

I understood what he was getting at. Both of us turned our heads away from one another, a heat of anger ending our conversation. It was then that I accidentally stumbled over a rock. My bad leg hit the ground and I cried out in pain. I would've fallen, had Nathan not caught me.

"Are you all right?" Nathan asked.

I wiped away involuntary tears. "Yes. Thank you."

"You're welcome."

I regained my footing and we started to walk again.

"Look…" Nathan started again. "You're right, I can't justify stealing. But we are in an enemy Nation that brought us here against our will. If there's a Nation to steal from, these guys are it."

"That is a valid argument." I noted. "…I don't like it. But, for this time, I'll allow it."

Nathan sighed, relieved.

But a question arose in my mind when I peered back at my leg.

"If you're really going to steal, how will you do it when I can't even walk?"

That got Nathan thinking. "Hmm. That's a good question."

We both thought on that a while. I came to an idea.

"What about the markets?"

Nathan simply gave me a questioning look.

"Most cities are filled with merchants and marketplaces." I explained. "Farmers, hunters, all sorts of people that sell food. They usually take their products out in the streets or the market where everyone can see them. We could easily take some from them without them noticing much."

Nathan shook his head. "That's just it though. They're where everyone can see them. We would get caught for sure."

"Wearing that, you will." I confirmed as I gestured towards his garments. "That just screams 'robber'."

"What do you suggest I do then?" He asked me. "I don't have any other clothes."

"Well, you could trade those horrid things for some other clothes." I told him. "That's what I did."

"Yes, but there's a difference between a princess's attire and mine." Nathan commented. "First of all, I need these. I need camouflage. It's a part of my life. If I don't have it, I'm dead. Also, who is going to take these?"

He had a very good point. I pondered on what he could do, not coming up with anything. "Umm, I'm not sure."

"You are right though." Nathan replied. "I'll get caught in these if *I* go out there."

Something nicked at me when he said "I".

"But…" He continued. "If a certain peasant-clothed girl could…"

"Why?" I suddenly interrupted. "Why do *I* to do the stealing?"

"We don't have many options." Nathan reminded me. "You can't be far from my side and I can't be stealing in these clothes."

"Nathan!" I complained, not wanting to steal.

"We need food, Sophia." Nathan reasoned.

And so…Nathan persuaded me to perform a robbery.

"I can't believe I'm doing this!" I whispered angrily at him as we neared a city. It was late morning and hundreds of people were in the marketplace. It would be extremely easy for us to take what we needed and then disappear.

Only I didn't want to.

"I can't do this! I've never stolen in my entire life!" I nearly begged Nathan.

"Oh, that has to be a lie." Nathan muttered. "It's okay. It'll be quick. It's not like they're starving. We are. Just some food. You're hungry, aren't you?"

Just the word "hungry" made my stomach growl.

"Yes." I groaned. "But I can't do this! How am I even going to take something with this leg?!"

"You have a staff." Nathan pointed out.

"I'll stick out!"

"No, you won't." Nathan argued.

"Oh yes I will!" I argued back. "No cripples go to markets! They send someone like their children or spouse! Everyone will notice me and then I'll get caught!"

"Even if they do notice you, they won't know you're Princess Sophia." Nathan reasoned. "They'll only know if you talk to them too much. Just take what we need and hobble away. I'll be watching you every moment."

I almost began to cry. "Nathan, I'm scared! I cannot do this!"

Nathan then put his hands on my shoulders and gently massaged them. His soft touch brought instant, soothing pleasure. I relaxed as he continued.

He whispered in my ear. "You'll be okay. Just go in, snatch something while the merchant is talking with someone and once you have a small meal, just walk out of there."

I was only half-listening to him. I was concentrating more on his incredible, angelic hands that sent the comforting vibrations through my upper back. Ever since we had crashed the carriage after escaping Mirrac castle, I had been extremely sore, but it seemed as if he was healing my aching body.

"Don't talk to anyone unless they speak to you first. If they do, make the conversation brief. If it's going on for too long, just give an excuse that you have to continue shopping because you need to get home to your family or something."

"Mmm-hmm." I moaned in acknowledgment. I still wasn't really listening.

Nathan stopped massaging. The soothing sensation stopped. My spirit fell a bit right there.

"Are you better?" Nathan asked me.

I took in a deep breath. "I am, yes."

His eyes smiled at me. "You can do this."

I sighed. "Yeah."

Nathan nudged me a bit towards the city. "Now, go get us some food."

I headed for the city. I walked in. I found the market. Easy.

But I was sweating. I was nervous.

I glanced around for Nathan, trying to find an encouraging gesture or something.

I couldn't find him. My spirits began to diminish.

I was in a Mirracian city, seemingly alone, and had to get some type of food without getting caught. If I did get caught, that most likely would mean capture by Seth.

I began to become depressed. *"What am I doing here? I have no experience with this. I'm a princess. Not a thief. How am I going to do this? What will the Shepherd think of me? I shouldn't just sin like this. Doesn't the Shepherd say He will provide for all our needs?"*

Suddenly, a pebble skipped across the dirt in front of me. I looked to where the pebble had come from. It was just a shadowy storage area beside a small building.

"Who threw that?" I wondered.

"Psst!" I heard Nathan whisper. The sound came from behind a box in the storage area. I glanced around to make sure no one was watching. Everyone seemed busy with their shopping. I nonchalantly made my way over to it. I went behind the box.

No one was there.

"What the?" I questioned, looking around for Nathan. "Nathan? Nathan?"

"Right here." He whispered behind me.

I turned around to find him hiding behind another box. That confused me. I thought for sure that the voice came from behind the first box.

"Can you throw your voice?" I asked him.

He gave me a perplexed expression. "What? No. Are you ready to do this or not? Standing around like you're lost is not the way to steal stuff."

"I want another back-rub." I told him.

The perplexed expression grew. "You want a what? No. Get us some food then you can get another back-rub."

"But I'm really sore!" I complained with a hushed voice.

"Go and get the food!" Nathan hissed quietly.

I growled a bit at him, but I obeyed and walked back out into the market.

"How do I even start?" I wondered. I approached a counter and sat there for a while, puzzled at how I was going to steal from it.

Apparently, I was standing there, eyeing the food for so long that someone noticed.

"Do you need some help?" An older boy asked me.

My head snapped up to see him at my side. He was quite a handsome young man. A little older than me. Probably even older than Nathan. Nathan's words suddenly rang in my head: *"They'll only know you if you talk too much."*

I had two options: ignore the dashing and eager-to-help man or change my dialect. I chose the latter.

"Oh, yes. Thank you." I smiled, talking in a slightly Mirracian tone. I also lowered my voice so as to further disguise my Ferandaron accent. Mirracians had more proper sounding voices.

I had always thought it was very attractive. Most Ferandaron girls do. He smiled back at me and dug some money out of his pocket.

"How much for a melon?" The young man asked the merchant.

"Three bronze tiukes and an emin." The merchant replied.

The young man counted out the money. The merchant handed him a good sized melon. The young man then handed the melon to me.

I gazed at the fruit in my hands and was utterly dumbfounded. There was no stealing involved! I just told the man I needed some help and he paid for a meal that could keep me and Nathan both going for several days.

"Are you feeding a family too?" He asked me while I stared at the melon. "I could get some more food for you if you're in need of some."

Oh. My. Goodness.

The Shepherd provided through this young man.

"You're so kind." I whispered.

And so the kind stranger bought me an entire meal that could have fed ten men. The only problem was that I couldn't carry any it with one hand, so he offered to carry it for me to my home.

That was problematic. My home was Ferandar.

"So where do you live?" He asked with a smile.

"What do I say?" I pondered.

"Oh, you've been enough help." I said, masking my nervousness with a friendly smile. "I can take care of them."

He laughed and shook his head. "Oh, no. You're in no condition to carry these. How will you even do it?"

"He's got me there."

"Well, that is true." I muttered.

"So where's your house?" He asked again.

"Don't panic! Don't panic! Tell the truth!"

"I actually don't live here." I spoke quietly as I nervously played with my hair.

"Oh, I know that." He replied.

"What?" I thought.

"What?" I said.

"I've never seen you around here before and I'm certain I would have noticed someone so beautiful." He explained.

I began blushing. "Oh, well…"

"So, are you getting ready for the festival? Is that why you came here?" He asked me.

My ears tweaked at that. "Festival? I didn't know of any festival."

"You didn't?" The young man sounded a bit surprised, but excited to talk about it. "It's going to be great! There will be hundreds of people there, with games and plays and dances and buffets and all sorts of stuff! You should come. It's tomorrow night after sunset."

I loved the sound of it.

"If I can, I will." I promised with an excited smile.

While the young man was carrying the groceries, he gave a small bow. "My name is Dev. What's your name?"

I curtsied (as best as I could) in response, but I didn't know what to say my name was. I stuttered helplessly, trying to think of something other than "Sophia".

"I'm uh…My name…My name is…" My mind raced rapidly, but I wasn't finding any name.

Dev chuckled. "Did you forget your name?"

I laughed nervously. "I, uh, must have."

Then something came to me.

"Anne! My name is Anne." I finally lied.

"Well, it's nice to meet you, Anne." He replied. "Now, what city do you live in?"

I didn't want to lie again. "Oh, just in the northern part of the Nation." When I said "Nation", I meant Ferandar. Dev seemed to be all right with that and we began talking as we made our way out of the city.

"Is that true?" I questioned as we walked out of the gates and onto the dirt path. "I never knew that. I always assumed the rumors to be correct."

"Well, many people do." Dev replied. "But the Conguar isn't necessarily nocturnal. It surely isn't a hunter. It likes to sit and wait for its prey. It usually rolls itself up in a ball to look like a big rock. Once something comes by that it thinks it can eat, it snatches it."

"Better watch out for rocks, then." I concluded.

"Indeed." Dev agreed. Then he stopped walking.

I turned and gave him a questioned look. "What is it?"

He was glancing down the road with a perplexed expression. "Where are you going?"

"Uhh, my city." I answered timidly.

"This path leads southwest. I remember you said you lived in the northern part."

I laughed nervously. "Oh right! Clumsy me! We better turn around."

Dev believed me and he began to wait for me to catch up with him to walk down the other path. I wasn't exactly sure how I would get him to go away or to convince him I needed to go southwest.

Then I saw that I didn't have to.

I never heard him. I never saw anything that reminded me he was still watching.

All of a sudden, I spotted Nathan fall out of a tree and land on Dev. They both rolled a bit, causing dust to fly up into the air. They also happened to crush some of the food. Eventually, they both jumped up to face each other.

Dev's face was full of panic and fear, but they were controlled. Nathan seemed like himself.

"Anne, run!" Dev screamed at me, taking out a knife. "Run!"

Before I could react to what Dev was saying, Nathan disarmed Dev, punched him several times in the gut and face, knocked him to the ground, and gave him a good kick to the head. The poor man was unconscious.

"Was that really necessary?" I asked Nathan angrily. "He was a very decent and good person."

Nathan turned to me. "Why are you still talking like that?"

For a moment, I didn't understand what he was saying. Then it came to me that Nathan was referring to the accent I was still using.

I had forgotten about it.

"Oh, right." I said, in my normal tone and dialect.

"To answer your question, I think it was perfect." Nathan commented. "Now he'll think that I was some murdering bandit that stole the food and you. He'll forget about you and we can move on without any ties to anyone here."

I grumbled a bit, but I couldn't deny that he was right. Had Dev known who I truly was, I don't know what he would have done.

Nathan carried the food as I walked with my staff. We traveled a ways and then camped in the forest where we weren't likely to be spotted and had our dinner.

It was amazing! Fruit! Bread! Unusually good lamb! I delightfully began to consume as much as I could until Nathan ordered me to save some for the rest of the trip. It was then that I noticed that Nathan had only had a small portion. I asked him to eat a little more but he refused.

He was used to hunger. He could deal with it.

Korhn ate until he was stuffed. I also awarded him with treats if he did tricks for them. He even screeched and threw his arms up, looking like he was surprised or afraid.

Nathan had told him I wanted to see him do it. It was hilarious!

After we stored the food away, we sat around a small fire Nathan built. I cleared my throat, wanting to get Nathan's attention.

He glanced at me. "Yes?"

"Time to hold to your word." I said as I moved closer to him. With the help of my staff, I sat myself down right in front of Nathan and threw my hair over my shoulder so it wouldn't interfere.

"Are you serious?" He questioned. "I never swore or promised that I would give you one."

"But you *said* you would." I reminded him. "Did you not?"

"Yes. What does that matter?"

"If you said it, you should treat it as a promise or a vow, unless you cannot fulfill it." I told him.

"And why would I do that?" Nathan growled, annoyed.

I turned to face him.

"Because it's the right thing to do, Nathan." I said with a smile.

His eyes flickered. I had used his own saying against him.

"Fine." He grumbled.

Then, his hands were gently placed on my shoulders and the soothing massage returned. I let the sensation flow through me and ease my stressed and tense body.

"Oh my goodness, you are amazing." I complimented him with my eyes closed. "This is better than my servants in Ferandar. How did you learn this?"

Nathan chuckled a bit. "Practice. I helped a girl with a bad back."

That sent off something in my mind.

"He's been with a girl before? I wonder for what reason." I wondered. Of course, I couldn't just ask him that. Up until now, I had allowed my curiosity to run rampant rather than my manners. I had pressed Nathan with question after personal question. Most of them without consideration for his feelings, which, from what I could tell, were prominently painful.

So, rather than just ask him a question he may not have wanted to answer, I decided to talk around the subject. This would let Nathan reveal things when he felt comfortable to do so.

"Oh, that was very kind of you." I said. "She must have loved this too."

"Yeah, she did." Nathan said with a laugh. "Of course, the first time I tried to help I came on really strong and it only made her back worse. I got better over time."

"Oh my. Well, I'm glad you helped her. Was she a good friend of yours?" I asked nonchalantly.

"The best. She's like family to me." He responded.

"Do you still see her from time to time?"

"No." Nathan spoke quietly. "I haven't seen her in years. She got caught while stealing. She's in prison now."

"I'm sorry." I told Nathan.

Nathan shrugged. "She's not dead. Just locked up."

"Why didn't you gct caught?" I questioned.

"I wasn't with her. I was chasing after Leos at that time."

"Why did you travel with her in the first place?" I asked, finally getting to the question I truly wanted answered.

Nathan was quiet for a while, silent as he massaged my back.

"Because we were scared to be separated. We were all we had left after Leos destroyed everyone."

"She's part of his tribe!" I concluded in my thoughts. *"They were the survivors! Wait! She might have been the one who saved Nathan's life! It all makes sense!"*

"Was she the friend that helped you after Leos slashed you?" I asked him.

Nathan continued to rub my shoulders as we sat there in silence. Every now and then, the fire popped. I waited for a while and finally concluded that Nathan was not going to tell me, when…

"Yeah." He whispered.

I could tell by the tone in his voice that he didn't want to talk anymore. I didn't ask any other questions.

Nathan stopped rubbing my back and I thanked him for it.

Before long, we were both laying down for sleep. But instead of resting, I was thinking. I was thinking on how Nathan must have had such a sad life. To have someone so dear to him betray him and kill his tribe, to have his parents murdered, to have such a hate that he would travel across Dedonaarc and possibly the rest of the world to hunt down Leos.

So much sorrow, so much bitterness. I deeply pitied him.

But there was also something else I saw in that boy. I saw morals. Selflessness, courage, intelligence.

He had so much promise, so much potential.

I turned on my side so I could look at him. He lay asleep with Korhn huddled in his strong arms.

"What if I could turn you into a knight?" I wondered to myself. *"You could live at the palace and become a great man."*

Many of these thoughts came to my mind while I lied in the soft grass. Then another came.

"Father would never allow that."

It was true. He abandoned Nathan in Mirrac. Never would he let him live in our palace.

I dwelt on these thoughts until sleep finally took me.

The next morning came very quickly. Nathan woke me up around daybreak.

"Don't you ever sleep in?" I asked groggily. I began rubbing my eyes.

"No." He replied frankly. "Let's get moving."

As we continued our travels, I began pondering on what Dev had told me.

"Nathan?" I broke the silence.

"Yes?"

"Can I see the map?"

"Why?" He glanced back at me.

"I want to know where we are and how much longer it will take to get home." I replied. It wasn't the true reason I wanted to see the map, but it wasn't a lie either.

Nathan dug in his pack and handed me the map. I examined around the area where we were.

"This map has no cities on it." I said.

"Nope." Nathan confirmed. "Just the Nations."

"Well, we need to find a map with cities." I told him.

"Why? We don't need to know where the cities are. Just where the border of Ferandar is."

"But what if we're heading the wrong way?" I questioned.

"We're not. We're heading southwest. More west than south, just like you said. I know where I'm going."

I didn't doubt that he knew exactly where to go, but I wanted to go to the festival that Dev had spoken of. Yes, it was foolish of me, but ever since the war with Mirrac began, there weren't many big festivals in Ferandar.

"I want a map with cities." I told him, but with a kind voice.

Nathan turned around.

"What are you planning?" He started to see through me. "I'm your guide, I'm leading you home. If you could get home by yourself, you wouldn't need me, would you?"

I shuffled my good foot nervously. "I'd need protection."

Nathan nodded at that. "Okay, that's true. But why do you want a map with cities?"

I bit my lip. *"Now's the time to tell him."*

"I want to go to the festival." I mumbled.

Nathan's eyes widened. "What did you say?"

I played with my hair. "I want…to go to the festival."

"What festival?" Nathan questioned.

"The festival at Navil."

"Navil?"

"That's Dev's city." I pointed out. "You did know that, didn't you?"

"Who is Dev?" Nathan threw his hands open.

"The young man that bought the groceries for us." I explained. "He was very kind, remember? Then you kicked him in the face like he was a scoundrel. His city, Navil, is having a festival tonight."

"You mean the city that's behind us?" Nathan pointed his thumb behind him. "The opposite way of Ferandar?"

"Well, it's not *far*." I reasoned.

Nathan sighed. "We're not going."

"Please?"

"No." Nathan growled louder.

"But maybe we could-"

"Are you out of your mind?" Nathan cut me off. "Do you remember that we are in Mirrac? Enemy territory? They want to **kill** me and **capture** you. We are being chased by an assassin while the whole stinking Nation is searching for us. We couldn't even fool a physician. Knowing all of this, you want to go to a festival?"

I stared at the ground. "Yes, I do."

"Oh, I can't believe this." Nathan threw up his arms and turned away from me. "This is ridiculous! We're running from a murderer and you want to go and dance?"

Suddenly, I got angry. Nathan didn't know any of my reasons.

"Yes, I do!" I shouted at him. That surprised Nathan and he turned to face me with a bewildered look.

"I want to dance!" I snarled. "I haven't danced in a long, long while and I love to dance! I love festivals and I will not be rebuked because of that!"

"But Princess-" Nathan tried to reason.

"No! We are going to that festival!" My shouts grew louder. "You are going to take me and by the heavens, I am going to dance!"

Nathan tried to quiet me down. "Okay, okay...I'll take you to the festival."

At that, my anger was gone.

"Eeeeeeeeee!" I squealed. I nearly began jumping up and down. "I'm so excited!"

Nathan snickered.

"What?" I asked, still in a great mood.

"We may be going 'by the heavens' but I don't think the sky is going to help you dance with that leg."

I instantly stopped and realized what he said. How would I be able to dance with a broken leg?

I could have cried right then, but instead...

"You know, you just ruined my entire day." I whimpered to Nathan.

"Good, because you did the same to me." He answered back with a cruel tone in his voice.

I didn't want Nathan to think of me as a weak little girl...

But that comment hurt me.

NATHAN

This was not going to work. I could see it all the way from the shelter of the forest.

But I didn't say that. I had already hurt Sophia enough. I had seen how my angry words had upset her earlier that day.

That would make anyone feel heartless.

Sophia probably thought of me as heartless.

I dismissed that from my mind. Why did I need to worry what she thought of me? Better for her to detest me than like me. I had felt that, for a little while at least, she had begun to grow attached to me and I did not want any of that with this girl.

It might just give me hope for a happy life.

A happy life died with my people.

"So how are we going to do this?" I asked her.

"Easy. We just walk in." Sophia told me quietly.

I didn't want to make her feel bad again, but there was something that I needed to point out to her.

"Princess, if we go in there, there's no doubt that we will be caught." I told her yet again.

"Why are you such a pessimist?" She smiled at me.

"What did you call me?" I asked her.

"A pessimist." She repeated.

I had no idea what the word meant, but it sounded foul and insulting.

"You know, I'm sorry that I may have treated you badly, but I don't need to be called that." I glared at her.

She gave me a confused look. "A pessimist? But that's what you are in every situation we've been in."

"I am not." I growled.

She gave me a blank face. "You don't know what it means, do you?"

I felt really stupid right then. Pessimist did not mean what I thought it did.

But for some reason, I lied to her.

"Of course I know what it means." I scoffed. "I'm not an idiot."

Sophia smiled sinisterly. "Then what does it mean?"

"I'm not going to say it out loud." I said, obviously not knowing what it meant. "It's inappropriate."

"It is not, you liar." Sophia hit me playfully. "You have no idea what it means."

"Then what does it mean?"

"Someone who always look at the downside of a situation." Sophia explained to me.

"That actually sounds a lot like me." I thought.

"Whatever." I responded. "So how are we getting in without being noticed, opmist?"

"It's optimist." Sophia corrected me. Then she laughed. "You know what 'optimist' means, but you don't know what 'pessimist' means? How does that work?"

"Who cares? I never went to school, okay?" I snarled. "Just enlighten me on how we're going to get in there and how people won't immediately shout and point at us."

She turned and examined me. "That's true. We won't get in with you like that. Could you just…take off the mask and cloak?"

She suggested very timidly, as if she didn't want to offend me or make me feel uncomfortable about shedding my thief garments.

"Without those, your attire seems very much like a regular peasant." She gave a nervous smile.

I glared at her. "No."

"Oh, please!" She begged. "Just for this time only! Then you go back to your disguise! Please, Nathan, please!"

I shook my head. "No, Sophia. Even if I wanted to, I'd be recognized."

"By who?" Sophia threw up her arms.

"Leos has probably told everyone what I look like. I need to keep the disguise on." I explained. It wasn't true, but I wanted to keep my mask on.

"But then we won't be able to go!" Sophia told me.

"Exactly. We should just move on." I began to walk away, relieved that I wouldn't have to go into a crowd of hundreds of people in an enemy Nation.

But I was stopped…

"Nathan! Nathan, look!" Sophia shouted excitedly. She ran over to me and yanked me back to our observation spot by my arm.

"What?" I asked her, annoyed. She pointed at some people entering the festival with an excited squeal.

I groaned.

There was a Hertuen. He was wearing his traditional veil and even wore a traditional hooded cloak.

"You've got to be kidding me." I grunted.

"Let's go!" Sophia yanked on my arm again.

"Wait." I pulled my arm back. "We can't just go running up there. We'll be seen. Besides, what do you expect us to do?"

"Steal his outfit." Sophia beamed. "It'll be perfect for you."

"What about the Hertuen?"

"I'm sure you'll figure that out." Sophia said. Without another word, she quickly hobbled off.

"Sophia!" I whispered at her. "Get back here! What are you doing?!" But she was already rushing to the gates of Navil. She zipped in without any hesitation.

I sat back, scratching my head.

"What am I going to do with her?" I groaned to myself.

Suddenly, Sophia came rushing out with the Hertuen. Sophia's countenance was completely different. She had the look of panic, fear, and desperation on her face. In turn, the Hertuen looked rather concerned.

I immediately knew what she was doing. She probably had told him that I was wounded or dying and I needed his help. She would bring him right to me and I would do the rest.

Not a bad plan. I must say that I was impressed. She had become quite deceptive when she wanted to be. I suppose I was rubbing off on her.

I proceeded to lay down so I looked like I was injured. I tried to plan what I would do after Sophia and the Hertuen arrived.

I couldn't come up with anything.

Sophia abruptly came into view, the Hertuen behind her.

"See?! He won't get up! Please help him!" Sophia shrieked to the Hertuen.

The Hertuen knelt down to me, immediately looking for signs of injuries or sickness.

Then I lifted my head up. "Hey."

The Hertuen blinked, rather surprised.

"Women, am I right?" I shrugged. "Always complicate things."

Then I punched him in the face.

The outfit was big on me. Also, it was very uncomfortable. Hertuens always put tradition before themselves and I couldn't help but wonder why.

I guess they were pretty selfless and focused more on the whole of their people. Then again, the Hertuen that I stole the traditional garments from wasn't exactly standing up for his Nation by coming to a Mirracian festival.

We entered the gate with no problem. The guards simply saw a Hertuen boy and a Ferandaron girl. Possibly a couple, but most likely not. The only reason I stayed close to Sophia was to make sure she was safe. Korhn had to be left outside. We didn't want Leos hearing of a man with a raccoon at a festival.

The festival was rather large. The whole city seemed involved. Torches were lit everywhere to brighten up the night. Small bands of string musicians were playing lively and upbeat music for the crowds of people who were all dancing in the city square. Puppeteers, magicians, and other stage-artists were entertaining folks here and there.

Food was everywhere. Meats, fruits, bread, you name it. There were even certain Mirracian delicacies that I had only heard of. The smells were utterly alluring, but I dared not leave Sophia.

After all, I was panicking.

We were surrounded by hundreds of Mirracians! It would only take one person to notice who we were to bring an army of Mirracians, or even worse, Leos.

I had to resist the urge to put my hand on my (also known as Jon's) knife every time a Mirracian got a little too close.

"Are you okay, Benjamin?" Sophia asked me. We both agreed to use fake names. Mine was Benjamin in honor of my father. Sophia's name was Anne.

"Oh, yes, I'm fine." I sneered sarcastically.

"Oh, come on." Sophia nudged me. "Have some fun!"

"Fun?" I whispered to her. "We're surrounded by hundreds of Mirracians and you want me to have fun?"

Her face sunk. "You just love to bring me down, don't you Nathan?"

My anger vanished. She even used my real name.

Guilt. I hated guilt. I felt terrible. It was true. That's what I had been doing.

"I'm sorry, *Anne*." I told her, emphasizing the name. "You're right. I'm sorry. I'll try to be better…*Anne*."

She smiled. She could tell I was being honest and she understood my emphasis on the name.

"I'm sorry, too." She nodded. "I know this isn't the place you want to be…Benjamin."

"Well, you certainly want to be here." I mentioned. "In fact, you lied to get in here. You condoned stealing to get in here, too. That was surprising."

I eyed her with a smirk. Sophia looked guilty.

"I do feel pretty bad about that…" She muttered. "But I *really* wanted to come here."

I gave a smile. "Well…I guess we should have some fun then."

An excited light shone through Sophia's eyes.

"Then come on!" She gave a squeal.

The music was joyous and loud.

The food was plentiful and delicious.

The people were happy and enthusiastic.

Why, it even brightened my paranoid mood. A little.

I sat down on a log I pulled up and watched Sophia. She had been scarfing down food (as had I, we were both starving), watching the jugglers and such, and now she was dancing to the music.

I marveled at her. She had a broken leg, yet she was dancing. Granted, it wasn't spectacular, but she was dancing. She was using the staff to keep her weight off of her bad leg.

She was talented, but as I said, it wasn't great. The woman had a broken leg. She was unable to dance freely and lively as others were.

Yet…I was entranced by her dancing.

I…don't know how to say it exactly…but I couldn't take my eyes off her. I was hypnotized.

She was absolutely beautiful.

Her dazzling blue eyes. Her stunning smile.

She was looking at me as well. She smiled even brighter when she glanced at me. She even began to blush, but she continued dancing.

When I finally noticed that she saw me watching her, I broke out of the trance and turned away.

"What are you doing, Nathan?" I raged at myself. *"That's the princess of Ferandar! What are you doing?"*

Suddenly, a hand grabbed my arm. I turned to see Sophia's celestial face.

"Benjamin! Come dance with me!" She urged me.

"Oh, no." I told her. "No, I shouldn't. I'll just stay-"

She pulled me to my feet. "Yes! I need help! Come dance with me!"

"She probably does need help", *"I am technically subject to her commands"*, *"I need to stay near her to protect her"*, I could have used any of those excuses to convince myself that I actually did not want to dance with her.

But I knew…

Oh, yes, I knew…

That I truly wanted to dance with her.

So I surrendered to her wishes and was pulled into the crowd of dancing people.

"Listen, Anne, I haven't danced in ages." I spoke nervously. "I don't even really know ***how*** to dance like this."

She gave me a smile. "Then I'll teach you. Here take my hand with your right hand."

I took her hand.

"And place your left hand on my waist." She instructed.

I did so.

Then she slowly began to sway. I did the same and we began to slowly dance together.

It didn't make any sense. The music was fast and upbeat, yet we were dancing slowly.

But…I didn't care.

I felt myself begin to move into the trance again as we swayed. Her eyes seemed to gleam like brilliant stars in the torchlight. I could see that she too was in the trance that she had been in before.

"She's definitely something special." I told myself. *"Whoever she marries will be a really lucky guy."*

Suddenly, Sophia took my hand from her waist and entwined her fingers between mine. I held her hand tightly, but not so tight that it would hurt her hand. Then we both moved closer to one another at the same exact moment. Our faces were so close that our noses touched. I could hear her heartbeat, I could smell the scent of the forest on her, and I couldn't do anything but stare into her heavenly eyes.

I was absolutely speechless.

So was she.

We danced and didn't say a word for what seemed like an eternity, yet at the same time, was so quickly over.

I could feel that neither of us wanted it to be over.

But it ended. It ended when I noticed that no one was dancing but us.

Everyone was watching us.

We were the center of attention.

The one place where we were *not* supposed to be.

I stopped dancing. Sophia became perplexed at my sudden halt, when she noticed the crowd as well.

Suddenly, a random guy began clapping and cheering for us. I could tell by the way he slurred and how he stumbled around that he had been drinking wine. A lot of wine.

But his clapping became contagious, apparently. Soon, everyone was applauding us, even though we had not exactly danced well.

As this happened, Sophia discretely nudged me with her elbow and then she curtsied.

I caught on and did a low bow. People were still applauding us, so I took Sophia's hand and casually made our way into the crowd.

We both sat down.

We said nothing for a long while and people continued with the festival.

"You...are a wonderful dancer." I said finally. "Even with a broken leg, that was incredible."

Sophia blushed and played with her hair. "Thank you. You were magnificent as well."

"I can see why you love dancing so much." I observed.

She smiled and nodded. "I do love it. It's a beautiful thing."

I so badly wanted to dance again with her, but I didn't ask her.

I just watched her. I observed her radiance.

I knew she knew I was watching her and she just continued blushing.

Everything was peaceful. Jubilant.

Until...

"Anne?" A voice asked.

Sophia's eyes widened. We both turned to see…

The boy that helped Sophia with the groceries before.

"Dev?" Sophia asked, amazed.

Dev gave a huge smile. "You're okay!"

He rushed up to Sophia and gave her a hug. Sophia was greatly surprised. I was jolted so much, I nearly stabbed the guy.

"I thought for sure that thief killed you!" Dev cried. "I'm so happy you're alive!"

Suddenly, Dev pulled away and gave Sophia a concerned look. "Did he hurt you? Did he…touch you?"

Sophia shook her head as she spoke in a Mirracian tone. "Oh no! No, he never laid a hand on me."

"How did you escape?" Dev asked her.

Panic came over Sophia's face. There was no way she could come up with a story that quickly.

If I didn't stop her, she would tell the truth.

We were already the center of attention in the dance, we didn't need any more.

"Excuse me, sir." I interrupted, changing my voice to sound deeper. "Please take your hands off of my sister."

Dev hadn't even noticed me. He turned and looked at me. Then he looked at his hands on Sophia's shoulders.

"Oh, I'm sorry!" The boy apologized, stepping away from Sophia. "I was just worried, you see I-"

Suddenly, he noticed my Hertuen attire.

"You're…a Hertuen." He observed. "Anne is a Mirracian."

"Yes, I am." I told him, improvising. "Is there a problem with that? Her mother is Mirracian. My father is Hertuen. They got married a while back. But who are you? You just waltz in here and bring up my sister's horrible encounter with that bandit?"

"Oh, yes I was just wondering how she-" Dev began to say.

I put up my hand to stop him. "Please! She doesn't wish to talk about that awful day! Don't speak of it!"

Dev immediately shut his mouth. Sophia began acting along with what I was saying.

"It was terrible." She muttered, shivering. "Terrible."

I put my arm around her. "Just forget it, Anne."

I glared at Dev. "You've already upset her. Leave us!"

Dev nodded and quickly walked away.

"We better go." Sophia whispered quickly after he left.

"You like him, don't you?" I asked her.

She snickered. "Jealous?"

I ignored her, but kept my gentleman act. I helped her to her feet and then, I offered my arm to her.

She placed her arm around mine and we strolled out.

That night, I couldn't sleep. What a strange thing it was. Butterflies were in my stomach and hope was in my heart. However, guilt was in my thoughts. I knew I liked Sophia. There was no doubt there. I couldn't even try to convince myself otherwise. But as I lied in the grass, staring up at the stars above me, I knew it was only dangerous and foolish to get my hopes up for someone like Sophia. She was a princess. What was I?

I let out a deep sigh. From that moment on, I figured I needed to stop sighing.

Because Sophia heard me *again*.

"Nathan? What's wrong?" Sophia whispered.

"Uh, nothing." I laughed. "Just…thinking. Go back to sleep."

Sophia gave me a nervous look and bit her lip. "I, uh, want to talk to you actually. Is that okay?"

I sat up. "Sure. What do you need to talk about?"

"I can't go to sleep. I keep thinking about our dance." She said timidly.

"Oh. Uh, to tell you the truth…" I replied. "I keep thinking about that, too."

She smiled. "I've never danced with anyone like that before, and I've danced with many princes before. My parents are trying to rush me into marriage, you see."

I lied back down, looking at the sky. "That must be hard."

She nodded back. "It is. They expect me to have one day with a prince and to love him forever. But this…was different."

"How so?" I asked her.

"I feel like…I know you." She confessed. "Like I could trust you with anything."

I took that in. "Well…sorry, Princess, but you're wrong."

"What?" Sophia asked, confused.

I sat up once again, locking eyes with her. "Sophia, you have known me for a couple days. Not years. Not months. Not even weeks. Days. We've talked here and there, but you don't know me. You certainly can't trust me. I am a man who takes things from people. A thief. You are the daughter of the leader of our Nation. You belong with a prince. Please don't do yourself a disservice by confiding in me. Once we get back to your castle, I'm dropping you off and going back to what I do best."

I could see in her eyes that she was saddened by what I told her. "Oh… Yes, that would be best. We should just get this done with and part ways."

Then we both remained silent for a while. I could tell she wanted to keep talking, but I just rolled and didn't say anything to her.

I did it to show her that I wasn't the right person for her. Korhn stared at me with sad eyes, but I ignored him too.

By the next morning, Sophia and I were back to normal. We even argued. And from that moment, I told myself I wouldn't ever dance with her again.

CHAPTER SEVEN
OLD FRIENDS

NATHAN

"We're here." I told Sophia the next morning as we hiked up a hill.

"We're finally back?" She asked me.

"Yes, your highness, we are." I let out a sigh of relief. "Welcome to Ferandar."

Sophia gasped as she saw the vast lands of Ferandar. We were really high up on the hill. Of course, Mirrac and Ferandar have very little difference at the border.

"Now…We just need to go through Stephen's territory." I groaned.

Sophia glanced back at me. "What? Stephen? Who's Stephen?"

I laughed at that. "You don't know Stephen? Stephen, 'the Prince of Felons'?"

Sophia realized. "Oh, yes. He stole directly from my father."

I nodded. "Yes and the only one who stole from his majesty and hasn't been caught by his guards."

"Two." Sophia corrected.

I turned to her. "What? No, he's the only one."

Sophia smiled and shook her head. "There's one more."

I couldn't think of anyone. Even Nila got caught.

"Who?" I asked her.

She pointed at me. "You are."

Me?

Yes, me.

I had stolen from his daughter's room. Of course, that was taken from me when I was captured.

But still, I had done it and wasn't imprisoned or killed…

Yet.

Then I realized something else. I had something far more important to William in my possession than gold.

His daughter.

I guess it was at that moment that I realized how powerful I was. I had the only daughter of the king of Ferandar with me. She trusted me and wouldn't believe that I would betray her.

I was the most powerful man in Ferandar.

Anything I wanted, it was mine.

Anything. Gold, power, Ferandaron land.

Mine.

"Nathan?" Sophia asked, watching me closely.

"Hm?" I snapped out of deep thought.

"You were just staring off there for a while." She told me. "You looked like you were thinking about something."

"I…was." I said slowly.

"What was it?" She asked curiously.

"Uhh…just of what could happen next." I said casually.

"Oh, with Stephen's territory?" Sophia asked.

"Yeah." I lied.

As trusting as she was, Sophia believed me. But for me, something jabbed me. My conscience and my greed were fighting. And my conscience was winning.

I felt guilt.

I hated…*hated* guilt.

"*What do you know?*" I growled at my conscience. "*With you, I've lived a terrible life. I've been starving for years. Now I have a chance for a good life. A life of riches.*"

"*Is life really about riches and comfort?*" Something inside replied back to me. "*If it is, why does anyone live with morals and honor?*"

I stopped. That was something my father had once said to me.

My father…

I then remembered what Sophia spoke to me.

"*Would you like a home where you don't have to steal?*"

As I stood there, staring at the Nation of my birth, I felt a deep conviction that I had not felt in a long time. And, unbeknownst to Sophia, I let tears well up in my eyes.

Maybe I *could* take Sophia's offer. If we lived to make it back to Iarrag, that is.

We began our walk down the large hill, finally in Ferandar again. But that didn't mean we were safe.

In fact, if Leos hadn't been a factor in Mirrac, we were now in far greater danger and risk.

Mirracian soldiers were strong and well trained, but I could get by them with stealth and speed.

Now we were in Stephen's land. He had dozens of spies that I wouldn't be able to catch sight of. Also, I couldn't hide, due to Sophia's injury.

We were bait for the shark. Truth was, I hadn't really thought about Stephen until this morning. And now, I knew that telling that to Sophia would only make things worse. I would be killed, Sophia would most likely be held for ransom.

I grew more discouraged as we walked further into Stephen's land. Sophia noticed.

"Okay, what's wrong?" She asked me firmly.

"Nothing, walk faster." I told her. I began to walk quicker and Sophia struggled to keep up.

"You're lying to me." Sophia said plainly.

"Yes I am. Walk faster." I said again.

"Nathan, stop!" Sophia jumped in front of me.

Honestly, I was surprised that she could do that. Then again, she did the same with her dancing.

She glared at me. "What is wrong? Tell me."

I sighed. I closed my eyes right then and listened.

Korhn suddenly hissed.

It was too late. They found us.

"Run!" I told Sophia as I picked her up.

Sophia let out a surprised shriek when I did so. "Nathan! What in the world is after us?!"

I ignored her. There were at least five of them after us. I could hear them in the bushes around us, chasing us down.

They were just as fast as me.

We were finished.

Suddenly, there was a sharp pain in my back.

"Augh!" I yelled as I tumbled to the ground. I dropped Sophia and we both rolled a small distance. I jumped up, ready to face them.

Too late. A fist flew into my face. I was back on the ground.

They were all beating me at once. Some of them were bashing at my face while others were stomping on me.

I heard Sophia screaming as I desperately tried to shove them off of me. I had some success and pushed some aside. I got to my feet and nailed one of them in his private area. He wheezed and fell to the ground, but the others tackled me and continued beating me until a shout rang out.

"Stop, you fools!" A familiar voice called.

The four that were thrashing me ceased. I turned my bloody face to see someone I didn't think I was ever going to see again.

Isaiah.

The brother of Stephen himself.

"Bring him to his feet." He said calmly. They did so. Then he glared at the ones around me.

"Idiots!" He spat. "Don't you think my brother would want him alive?"

The men around me muttered.

"Tie his hands!" He ordered. They obeyed.

"Sir, what about her?" One of them asked Isaiah. Sophia was struggling to get her staff.

"Be gentle with her." Isaiah commanded. "She comes too."

"Who are they?" Sophia whispered to me. They allowed me to walk next to her at Isaiah's order. They stayed a distance away, but kept a close watch on me.

"They're Stephen's men. All bandits or criminals of some kind. The leader is Isaiah, Stephen's younger brother."

"How do you know that?" Sophia questioned.

"I've run into these guys before." I explained. "Stephen…doesn't like me. Strike that, he hates me. He's had a deep grudge against me for several years."

Sophia let out a sad sigh. "Why does everyone have to hate you?"

"You tell me." I replied.

"…Did you know this would happen?" Sophia asked slowly.

"Well…yeah" I muttered.

"What?" She whispered angrily. "Then why did we come this way?!"

A very good question. I hadn't thought of a taking an alternate route until we were basically in Stephen's territory.

But I wanted to defend my pride, so I lied a bit.

"The only way around Stephen's area is by going through Oridion." I made up. "Would you have wanted that?"

"Yes, Oridion would be much better than this!"

"Going around would have taken much longer." I shot back. "May I remind you that we have a deadly assassin on our tail. We had a better chance coming this way."

"Oh, really?!" Sophia snapped sarcastically. "Yes, because this turned out so much better!"

"Quiet." I growled. Stephen's men were watching us even closer since we were yelling.

"Quiet? Quiet?! Nathan, why didn't you tell me about this?!"

"Scicolíetnociet." I growled again.

Sophia calmed down at that, seeing I was speaking in my native language.

"Enough, separate them." Isaiah told one of the men. I needed to say one last thing to Sophia.

I got close to her and whispered in her ear. "It'll be okay. Leos won't let us stay there and Stephen won't let us leave."

That seemed to frighten Sophia. "What? Leos? What are you talking about?"

"Just trust me." I told her as one of the men grabbed me and pulled me away. "Trust me. I'll be seeing you soon."

SOPHIA

We were split up. They took Nathan down another path and I was left with Isaiah and another man.

I walked right behind Isaiah and in front of the other man.

"If I may ask…" I said suddenly. I was asking permission to speak.

Isaiah turned and glanced at me. He was young-looking and had slick black hair and dark brown eyes. He wore the same kind of attire Nathan did, even the same mask, but the fabric was newer and cleaner than Nathan's.

I was relieved he didn't smell.

"Speak." Isaiah allowed.

"How did you meet Nathan?"

Isaiah stopped walking and glanced at the other man. "Geoffrey, take a walk."

"Yes, sir." The man behind me said and quickly ran off.

After he was gone, Isaiah turned to me. He removed his mask. He was just a boy. Probably younger than me.

"Nathan saved my life." He said to me. "I…was in a fire. My brother, Stephen, couldn't get to me. Nathan could and did."

"Where did you live?" I asked.

"North Ferandar."

"Your parents? Where are they?"

"Dead. Died a long time ago."

"How did you survive?" I asked him. "How did you…get food?"

Isaiah laughed a bit. "So many questions. Why so curious about me?"

I shuffled my feet. "Forgive me. I don't know much of the bandit life."

"Eh, not much of a life to live." Isaiah shook his head. "How did we survive? How does any orphan survive? Steal. That's how we started. Just what we needed. That's all that we stole. Then Stephen wanted more. Like every man who has nothing. We wanted to live like the people we stole from. So, we gathered others who had the same desires. We gathered ten, then twenty, and more and more. We became quite a problem for wealthy Ferandarons. Then, after my brother had that idiotic idea to steal from the king, William sent his army to wipe us out. Many died. A fire was started at our hideout. I was trapped. Then someone came…someone I had never met before. He saved me, even though he never even knew me…"

I smiled. "Nathan is like that."

Isaiah smiled as well. "Yes. My brother grew very fond of him very quickly. It helps that he saved me, of course."

"So why do you and your brother hate Nathan now?" I asked curiously.

"I don't hate Nathan." Isaiah said bluntly. "We're still on good terms, secretly. If Stephen knew, he'd be furious. I still see Nathan as a good friend."

"But back there you-" I began to say.

"I have to keep up appearances." Isaiah explained. "As I said, Stephen would be furious to discover my friendship with his worst enemy."

"So why are Nathan and Stephen enemies now?"

Isaiah couldn't help but smile. "Why else? A girl."

"A girl?" I breathed, somewhat startled.

Isaiah nodded, his smile slowly fading. He began to stare at the ground. "Yes. Stephen and Nathan loved the same woman."

"There's someone else." I concluded gravely.

Suddenly, pain.

That's what I felt. But confusion followed.

"Pain? Why pain? I should be happy for him. He...deserves someone special."

But the pain was still there. It was a...longing. I instantly shoved that feeling away.

"No, no, stop that. You just need to get home. No attachments. No attachments."

But then...the dance we had flooded my memory.

"Stop that! Stop that now!"

I concentrated on Isaiah once again. He was still staring at the ground. "Where is she?" I asked slowly.

"Only in our memories." Isaiah said grimly.

My breath shuddered. I felt a terrible rush of pain for Nathan.

His entire tribe was murdered. Everyone he loved. By a man that was like family to him.

Then he fell in love...And now she was dead as well.

"Did...did you know her?" I asked as Isaiah began walking again.

"Ruth? Oh, yes." Isaiah nodded as I followed him. "She was originally promised to my brother."

"Oh dear." I gasped.

"You got that right." Isaiah knew what I was referring to. "Nathan really charmed her. She decided she didn't love Stephen anymore and they ran away together."

"Hence the hatred for Nathan." I concluded.

"Basically." Isaiah replied.

"If I may ask, how did Ruth die?" I questioned him.

"I mean no offense, but that's not my business to be speaking about that." Isaiah told me. "That conversation should be with either my brother or Nathan."

Mixed feelings whirled up inside of me again. It was like a small storm inside me. I wasn't sure what to think.

But I knew one thing:

"Nathan's lived a horrible life." I whispered.

"We all have." Isaiah told me. "We're hated for just trying to live. We steal to eat. People with 'class' and power want us dead for that. If some just shared, we'd all be content."

"With all due respect." I cut in. "King William has seen to it that good, honest jobs are available to any man or woman throughout Ferandar. It's not like there's a dearth for work. Nobody here *has* to be a bandit. You just choose to, for whatever reason."

"My, you are bold." Isaiah chuckled. "I could beat you for words like that, you know."

I took in a breath. That was the last thing I needed at that moment. However, due to Isaiah's laughter and cheery tone of voice, I suspected he wasn't actually threatening me.

"Ah, don't look so scared." Isaiah said, looking back at me. "I'm not the type. However, just for the record, my brother very much is. Hold your tongue around him. And as for what you said…"

Isaiah grew serious. "I guess you're right. I thought of a couple excuses to debate your point, but they're only that: excuses. They're not real reasons. I suppose I may have bought into the thief's justifying mindset. Maybe we could change if we really wanted to."

"Would you?" I pondered, genuinely curious.

Isaiah thought about it. "No. Because I don't want to. I'd bet no one in our little gang would. We could change, but I think we're all too bitter and angry about the hands we were dealt. So we won't, your highness."

I sighed. I had hoped that the opposite answer would have come.

"I'm sorry you think that way." I said sadly.

"I'm not." Isaiah replied coldly.

Suddenly, I caught on to something. "You called me 'your highness'… You know who I am."

Isaiah nodded. "You reek of royalty."

I blinked at that. I wondered what such a peculiar statement could mean. I was at a loss of what to say.

Isaiah suddenly spoke up again, his tone much different. "What about you, Princess Sophia? You've asked so many questions about me. Tell me how you got involved with Nathan."

"He saved me." I smiled. "From Mirrac."

"What a guy." Isaiah laughed. "You could almost call him a hero."

A hero.

"I suppose you could." I muttered. "He does quite a lot of saving for a thief."

"Ironic, isn't it?" Isaiah said.

Then he stopped walking.

"We're here."

NATHAN

I was taken to Stephen's hideout. It was amazingly camouflaged in the forest. I was shocked at how much it had grown since the last time I had seen it. Then again, it was about a year ago. They were just small shacks hiding in the shadows of the trees, but there were dozens of them. Maybe up to fifty of them.

"So, where to, gentlemen?" I asked the three men around me.

"Silence." One told me. I expected so. No doubt Stephen told everyone about my "treachery".

I was brought to one that seemingly was designated as the prison-house. I was tied to a post in the middle of a wooden cell. Korhn was thrown in with me. At least they kept him alive…for now.

"Hey, Nathan." I heard from the cell next to me.

"No way." I coughed with a smile. I turned. "Hey, Jon."

There he was. Brown-haired, blue-eyed Jon. Tied to a post, just like me.

"Where's Sophia?" He questioned me almost instantly.

"Stephen has her." I informed him. "Don't worry, he won't hurt her. He'll just sell her to the highest bidder."

Jon slumped down. "Great. That means he'll sell her to Seth. Seth has more wealth than anyone in Dedonaarc."

I knew that as well. "Yeah. Where are the king and queen?"

"Captured by Mirracian guards." He stated, his face full of sorrow. "I failed them. I came to get help, but was captured by your buddy here."

I laughed. "My buddy? You think a friend would put me here? No, he wants me dead."

Jon gave a smirk. "So even bandits want to kill each other? Heheh, that's funny."

I ignored him and spotted Korhn laying down to rest. I followed his plan and tried to get as comfortable as I could while sitting up. I closed my eyes to get some sleep when Jon noticed.

"What are you doing?" Jon asked. "Praying?"

"Oh, ouch." I winced as I opened my eyes. "That kind of struck my conscience a bit. Um, no, I was going to try and sleep."

"Sleep?" Jon raised an eyebrow.

"Prayer probably would be a better option, though, I agree." I nodded at him. "You get right on that."

Jon narrowed his eyes. "Can't you get us out of here?"

"No."

"Why not?" Jon grunted. "You got us out of a Mirracian dungeon of stone and iron. Why is this wooden one such a problem?"

I sighed, a little tired that I had to explain the difference.

"It's not the structure that's the problem." I glanced over my shoulder at him. "It's who guards it. These are my people. They know everything about my tricks and skills. It would be like trying to escape from myself. We'd be caught for sure."

"So you're just giving up? Not even going to try?" Jonathan snarled. "That's pathetic."

"Says the guy who abandoned his king and got captured by 'scum'." I retorted rudely.

"…That was unnecessary." Jon grumbled.

"So was your comment." I shot back. "I'm a bandit. Not emotionless."

"Okay, you're right. That was wrong of me." Jon apologized. "I just want to get out of here so we can help Sophia. Without us, they're going to ship Sophia off to Seth. I can't let that happen."

"You really care about her, don't you?" I asked Jon.

"What?" Jon sounded surprised "Well, certainly nothing romantic, but yes. She means a lot to me."

"Hey, I would understand if you like her." I told him. "She's a very special girl."

"I don't care for her that wa-" Jon suddenly paused. "…Wait, do *you* like her that way?"

I remained silent for a long while. "I'll help you get her out of here."

"Great." Jon breathed. "Can we go now?"

"No." I said. They had taken my knife and even if I had gotten Korhn to chew through the ropes that bound my hands, I would still have to get out of my cell. The door was locked with two latches on the top and bottom of the door. Even if I could reach them, they had taken my pick. I had no way of picking the locks.

"We have to stay here for a bit." I told him.

"Until when?"

"I don't know." I confessed.

"Nathan, you have to try!" Jon was losing patience. "Get to work, you idiot!"

"Back to the insults, are we?" I glowered at him. "I told you, I *can't* do anything about it."

"That's just laziness!" Jon accused. "What if your life was on the line? I'm sure you would find a way then!"

"My life *is* on the line!" I began to raise my voice. "You think I'm here on a social visit? Stephen is going to have my head."

"Then save yourself." Jon challenged. "And save us."

"Not right now."

"Why not?" Jonathan questioned angrily.

"At nightfall. That will be the best time." I commented.

"That could be too late!" He raged.

"Do you want to die?!" I yelled back. That silenced him.

I calmed down a bit. "We have no chance with the sun out. *NO* chance. At nightfall, we have something. We'll go then."

Jon kept his fierce gaze on me. "How?"

"I'm expecting someone." I answered.

LEOS

"Finally." I thought to myself. I had tracked Iveslo and the Ferandaron princess to the Mirracian-Ferandaron border. I wasn't even a day's journey behind them when word had come to my ears of the princess of Ferandar being auctioned by a prominent thief of Ferandar. It was likely that Iveslo was still with her. Fortune was, for once, on my side. Iveslo and the princess had eluded my grasp by a hair's length. Iveslo would be dead and the princess recaptured had it not been for the ill-luck I was dealt. The Conguar had delayed me. Afterward, the putrid vermin surrounded me because of the brat. I was covered all over with scratches and bites from the horde of raccoons. I was sore and irritated because of the rodents. But now I had Iveslo. Captured by one of his own, Iveslo and the girl were now both within my reach.

That made all the scratches and bites worthwhile.

I reached the criminal's hideout and, once his lackeys knew whom I represented, I was brought straight to his quarters.

Seth was rich. They all knew it.

I entered to find a boy, sitting at a table with a several jewels and riches. I raised an eyebrow at the boy. He returned a defiant, proud glare.

"Where's Stephen?" I questioned.

"I am Stephen." The boy replied.

Compared to my size, the boy was a mouse. I laughed.

"You're just a child." I chuckled.

"Fool!" The boy grew angry. "I'm the most powerful criminal in all of Ferandar! How dare you?!"

I stopped laughing. "Very well, then."

The boy calmed himself. "What do you want, Mirracian?"

"The princess of Ferandar and a thief called Nathan." I told him. "This is by the order of Lord Seth himself."

The boy scoffed. "What do I care of what Seth wants? What do I get for this?"

I glowered at him. I had no money with me to offer him. I tried to intimidate him. "You get your life, your men's lives, and this pathetic hideout of yours."

"No." The boy responded. "I get to do whatever I want with them. They're mine and if you want them, you'd better learn some respect before I teach it to you."

"I could crush you." I snarled.

"And I could stab that pretty throat of yours." He folded his arms in defiance.

"You *will* give them to me." I pressed.

"No, I won't." The boy snapped back. "I don't care what you say. What I have said is final."

"You dare defy Mirrac?" I questioned him.

"I defy all, Mirracian." He smirked. "You don't scare me. Just try and take those two from me. I would kill you before you stepped into my hideout again."

I let out a deep breath. "We shall see."

I began to leave, as the arrogant child called after me. "That's right, you brute! Run away to your king and send someone with more brains next time!"

"*I'm going to kill him.*" I thought silently.

NATHAN

Time really moves slow when you want it to move fast. I hate it. More importantly, Jon hated it. He wouldn't...stop...talking.

"Nathan, she could be gone by now!" He exclaimed. "We have to go!"

"I told you!" I groaned. "It's too early. Stop worrying, he won't get the message out for a while. It'll be okay."

"How do we know he's even auctioning her?!" Jon panicked. "He may just have sent her to Mirrac! Didn't you see the bounties for you and her? They were huge!"

I lifted my head up. "There's a bounty for me?"

"Yes." Jon pressed.

"How much?"

"Why does that matter?"

"I'm curious."

"Um, fifty-thousand gold tiukes."

"Fifty-thousand *gold* tiukes?!" I gasped. "Whoa! That's huge! I didn't think I was that important."

"Would you focus?" Jon snapped. "All of Ferandar is at stake here."

"Okay, okay." I told him. "What was Sophia's?"

"Who cares?" Jon threw up his arms.

"I care." I scoffed.

Jon sighed. "It was something like sixty-thousand or seventy-thousand gold tiukes. Something around there."

I whistled. "That is a lot of money."

Then I realized something. "Wait a minute. You knew my exact bounty, but you didn't know Sophia's?"

Jon sort of just blinked nervously. "Oh, well I, uh, just was...curious."

"You were thinking about giving me to Seth." I accused.

"No!" Jon said quickly.

I glared at him.

He broke, guilt sprouting on his face.

"Well...maybe. But I wasn't the only one!" Jon defended himself. "King William brought it up."

"Of course he did." I grumbled. "That's real typical."

Then the door opened. Jon and I became silent. Three of Stephen's men walked in. One pointed to me.

"Him. Get him."

"Great." I thought. *"Time to go see my old pal."*

They brought me to Stephen's chambers.
They threw me inside and waited at the door. My hands were still tied.
Then I saw him. Stephen, the Prince of Felons.
He was around my size, but he was three years older than me. He had
sleek black hair, brown eyes, and some light beard scruffle. Also, he
had a long scar across his temple, courtesy of me.
He turned around from his map.
"Leave us." He told his men.
They left.
It was me and Stephen.
"Well, if it isn't my favorite bandit." Stephen sneered at me. "Nathan
the Hieun. I never thought you would be stupid enough to actually
come back here."
"Well, you know me." I smirked. "I don't think."
"Of course you don't." Stephen growled. "You didn't think about what
I would do when you took Ruth from me."
Pain. Instant pain. I bowed my head so Stephen wouldn't see the
anguish on my face.
"Oh, what's that?" Stephen mocked. "You look a little depressed. How
do you think *I* feel?!"
Suddenly, he slammed his leg into my face. I fell onto the ground with
my face throbbing.
"You piece of dirt!" Stephen howled at me. "I welcomed you in! I gave
you a home! I practically made you my brother!"
He stomped on my bound hands. I yelled out as I felt some of my
fingers break.
"And after all that, you just steal away my love like I'm nothing but
another imbecile to rob!"
He kicked my stomach. The wind was knocked out of me for a couple
minutes.
Stephen calmed down a bit. "Well, I guess that makes you the best
thief, Nathan. You've made yourself so heartless that you steal
whatever from whoever you want. Even those close to you."
"Steal?" I coughed. "If I remember correctly, she loved me back. It
was her choice too."

"You think I give a care?!" Stephen questioned. "She loved me until you came along!"

He kicked me again in the stomach.

I glared up at him after recovering from his strike. "But I...wasn't the one...who...killed her."

Suddenly, Stephen's face was full of agony. Sorrow. Remorse. Then...anger replaced them.

"It was an accident!" He raged. He then kicked me in the back. "It was *you* I was after! *You* did this! Not me!"

He then ran up and kicked me in the face again.

"It's your fault! Your fault!" He continued.

I groaned in pain. "Why are you doing this?"

"Why?! Stow it, Nathan! You know why! The same reason you're tracking that assassin: Revenge! You took something beautiful out of my life so now I'm making you feel just a piece of the pain."

"Don't you think I was in pain too?!" I asked him. "I loved her!"

But Stephen didn't listen to me. I heard him unsheathe a sword. He bent down to my level and put the sword to my throat.

"I'm going to kill you, Nathan." He snarled at me. "This is for taking away the only love I've ever known."

He was about to slice my throat, when...

The door opened.

"Sir?" One of Stephen's men asked.

"Can't you see I'm busy, you idiot?!" Stephen exploded.

"You're brother wishes to see you immediately." The man answered quickly.

Stephen calmed down. He let out a deep breath and pulled the sword away from my neck.

"Send him in." Stephen spoke quietly.

I couldn't believe it. Isaiah no longer owed me for saving his life. Stephen stood up and put his sword away as Isaiah walked in. Sophia walked in behind him.

Isaiah's eyes glanced on me and for an instant, I saw concern. I saw fear. But he acted as if he didn't even see me. I understood, and I commended him.

Sophia, on the other hand, dropped to my side. Even with her bad leg.

"Nathan! Are you okay?" She gasped.

"I'm okay." I muttered.

"What is it, Isaiah?" Stephen asked, ignoring Sophia and I.

"I brought you Princess Sophia as requested, brother." Isaiah spoke emotionlessly.

"A bit early, don't you think?" Stephen asked.

"No need to make a mess before the princess enters. Wait until after." Isaiah advised.

Stephen nodded. "Sounds decent enough."

They began speaking further. Sophia whispered in my ear.

"How are we getting out of here? Please tell me you have a plan."

"Sort of." I informed her.

"That's better than nothing. Do it." She ordered.

"Take him back while I talk with her highness." Stephen told his brother.

"Very well." Isaiah replied. He then walked over to me and violently dragged me to my feet.

"Move." He commanded. I obeyed as he pushed me. I knew it was all an act to keep Stephen satisfied. As soon as we got outside, Isaiah stopped pushing me.

"Thanks for saving me back there." I whispered to him.

"No problem." He told me. "I'm just glad I got there in time. You got a plan to escape?"

"You could say that." I mentioned. "Just keep close to your brother when it happens."

"Can do."

Isaiah escorted me back to the prison-house and let me in.

"You guys need anything?" He asked Jon and me as we stepped inside. Jon seemed baffled.

"Some food would be nice, if you could." I told Isaiah. "And something for my fingers."

"Don't have anything for your fingers, but I can get you food." He said.

"You got to tie my hands to the post again?" I asked Isaiah.

Isaiah looked at my bound hands. He cut them loose with his knife.

"Nah. You should be fine." He smiled.

"Thank you." I smiled back.

"I do have to put you in the cell, though." Isaiah mentioned.

"It would be unprofessional of you not to." I replied. Isaiah opened my cell door and locked it after I walked in.

"Hey, um, can I get loose too?" Jon humbly requested.

Isaiah looked to me. I gave a simple nod.

Isaiah opened Jon's cell and cut his bands. Before Jon could even get his hands loose, Isaiah walked back out, locked his door, and left the prison-house.

"What was that all about?" Jon questioned me. "I thought they hated you here."

"Luckily, not everyone." I chuckled. Then I laid down next to Korhn and stroked his back. I stroked him for a while until I began to feel a little drowsy. I was very tired and hurt.

Hurt in more ways than just physical. Walking down memory lane with Stephen wasn't exactly pleasant.

I just closed my eyes for a second and…

I opened my eyes. Night. It was night. Some stew was sitting in a pot next to me. I could tell it was cold now. I sat up and dipped my finger into the pot. Then I put my finger in my mouth and discovered that the stew was indeed cold, but really good. I scooped up the bowl and scarfed down all I could.

I sat back and let out a satisfying belch. I then turned my attention to the darkness outside. If we were going to try and get to Sophia, now was the time. I glanced over at Jon. He was fast asleep with his stew pot cradled in his arms.

It was a funny sight.

I was just about to wake him…when I felt it.

A rumble.

I began believing that it was just part of my imagination. That it was nothing.

But then it came again. I began to become unsure.

I put my ear to the ground.

Yes. The ground was rumbling.

I knew what that meant.

"Jon!" I yelled. He shook from his sleep.

"Wh-what? What is it?" He asked groggily.

"Get as far back as you can!" I ordered him. I could feel the rumbling becoming more powerful.

Jon quickly began to wake up and moved to the back of his cell.

He then could also feel the quaking. "What is that?"

"That is either our way out of here." I told him. "Or our destruction."

"What are you talking about?" Jon asked with fear in his voice.

The rumbling was now shaking the prison-house. We could hear faint trumpets in the distance. People outside began shouting.

Then one, clear sound rang throughout the entire building.

An elephant roar.

They were close.

I grabbed Korhn and shielded him against the wooden cell bars. "Not again."

Then it came. An elephant burst through the prison-house wall.

"What in blazes?!" Jon shouted, but his yell was lost in the cries and trumpeting that was coming from outside. The elephant continued charging and crashed right through the wooden structure that contained us. Jon dove out of the way as the massive creature nearly trampled him. Luckily, the elephant didn't notice either of us. It continued its stampede through the rest of the prison-house until it reached the other end.

"Let's go!" I told Jon. I got up with Korhn and ran out of the ruined prison-house.

"What is going on?!" He questioned as he came behind me. We then both witnessed the army of elephants rampaging through Stephen's hideout. They were killing all in sight. Many bandits fought, but most likely none had faced elephants before.

Fortunately, I had.

I turned to Jon. "We have to find Sophia before Leos does!"

"Who's Leos?" Jon shouted at me.

"Just find Sophia!" I groaned.

He nodded and we both ran for Stephen's chambers.

My plan was to avoid the elephants and just get to Sophia as fast as possible.

But like Nila always told me, I didn't think things through.

I was the main target of the elephants. When I approached, the massive animals would see me and charge for me.

Many were after me. I began to lead them in the opposite direction as I yelled to Jon.

"Keep going that way!" I pointed towards Stephen's chambers. "I'll deal with them!"

Jon didn't ask any questions. He ran off where I told him to.

"Korhn, you go hide! Now!" I told Korhn, who was hanging on to my shoulder.

For once, Korhn didn't argue. He leaped from shoulder and fled.

I glanced back at the speeding elephants that were chasing me. They were gaining on me.

"*Great.*" I sighed. "*How am I going to get rid of these guys?!*"

I found a dead bandit lying on the ground.

I quickly took his sword.

JONATHAN

I burst through the door.

"Jonathan!" Sophia cried happily. She was tied to a chair. Two bandits were there in the room as well. When they spotted me, they ran at me with weapons ready. I reacted instantly. I evaded the first bandit's blade and plowed my fist into his stomach. Without hesitation, I threw him into the other advancing bandit. They crashed into the wall and tumbled over.

I stole both of their swords.

"Close your eyes, Princess." I warned her.

She obeyed. I drove the swords through them.

I ran over to Sophia and began untying her. She opened her eyes.

"Are you all right?" I asked.

She nodded with a smile. "I'm so glad you're okay, Jonathan."

I smiled back and quickly untied her.

"What's going on out there?" Sophia questioned. The sounds of screaming and trumpeting were still blaring, even through the walls. The earth was shaking from the elephants stampeding.

"…No time to explain." I told her. "We need to go now."

We began making our way to the door, when it was opened.

The bald axeman of Mirrac walked in.

"Leos." Sophia breathed quietly.

"Oh, he's Leos." I noted mentally.

I held up both swords against him. He didn't even flinch. His eyes were fixed on Sophia.

"You're coming with me, your highness." He smiled.

"Not on my watch, filth!" Someone behind Leos yelled out.

Leos snapped his head around to see Nathan leap onto his back. Nathan was covered in blood, but it didn't seem to be his. He held a bloody sword in his hand and shoved it into Leos' chest.

"Gaaaaaaahhh!!!" Leos roared. He threw up his arms and seized Nathan.

I saw an opening.

I charged in, driving both of my swords through Leos' stomach.

"Nnnrrrrrrgggghhh!!" He crumpled to the ground, howling furiously through gritted teeth.

The giant had been brought to his knees.

"Run!" I told Sophia. I grabbed her hand and pulled her beside Leos.
"Nathan, come on!" Sophia cried out as I brought her to the door.
Nathan was standing above Leos. Leos was cradling his horrid
wounds.
"Do you remember them, Shiako?" Nathan asked in a vicious tone.
"My parents? This is how they felt before you brought the final blow.
Bleeding. Weak. Helpless."
"If you're going to kill me, then kill me, already!" Leos coughed up
blood.
"No." Nathan glowered. "I want you to suffer. Die slowly. Then, my
tribe, *your* tribe, will finally be avenged."
"Nathan, we can't stay!" I urged him.
Nathan's eyes turned back to me and Sophia.
"Remember? Elephants?" I shouted.
"Yeah." Nathan nodded.
We left Leos behind, bleeding out in Stephen's chambers.

We ran outside and found the war between bandits and elephants
still taking place.
"More elephants?!" Sophia shrieked.
"'More'?" I questioned.
"Go, both of you. Go!" Nathan instructed. "They're after *me*! I'll
distract them!"
Just as he told us this, an elephant came running our way. Another
followed it. Sophia was much too slow when walking so I hoisted her
up on my back and carried her. Nathan was running in a different
direction, waving his arms, trying to get the elephants' attention.
And just like that, the elephants followed after him, giving Sophia and
I a chance to escape.
I began running away from the battle.
"No!" Sophia argued. "They're going to kill Nathan!"
Suddenly, she jumped off of my back. Now was especially not the time
to stick around. I grabbed her arm before she could run after the
elephants.
"Princess, we must leave." I said to her urgently.
"No!" She shouted defiantly, trying to pull free from my arm. "Not
without Nathan! You have to help him!"

The elephants were now charging away from us. It was the perfect time to escape.

"Your highness, I'm not going to risk our lives for a thief." I told her firmly.

"He is *not* just a thief!" Sophia yelled. "He's a noble warrior!"

"*Have you gone insane?!*" I thought. "*He must've brainwashed her!*"

"I don't care what he is!" I shouted back. "We must go *now*!"

Sophia turned to me with an angry scowl. "You will help him! I *order* you to!"

I was shocked. Something had definitely changed with the way she viewed Nathan. Last time I saw her, she saw Nathan as just a thief who had shown some kindness. Now, she was convinced that he was someone that she could not just leave behind.

And she was going to risk both of our lives to save his. I let go of her arm.

I sighed. "As you wish, Princess. Stay out of sight."

Then I ran after the elephants, leaving Sophia behind.

"*This is crazy!*" I thought to myself. "*I'm leaving the wounded princess of Ferandar by herself with hundreds of thieves around! Not only that, but I'm leaving her to go save another thief! From elephants! How in blazes am I supposed to do that?!*"

I pushed those thoughts away and simply concentrated on the task at hand. I spotted the elephants crashing through a large hut. They were trying to reach the dozen thieves on top.

One of them was Nathan.

I went over my options. I didn't have many, but I had a good guess. Most animals didn't take too kindly to fire.

After finding two blades and some straw from one of the destroyed huts, I began striking the swords together to make sparks.

Within no time, I had a blazing torch.

I charged at the two elephants, shouting and waving the torch around.

It caught the creatures' attention. One of the elephants simply began backing up. The other reared up on its hind legs.

Both were trumpeting loudly.

Nathan saw his opportunity and leaped onto the elephant that was now on its hind legs. He took a sword in hand and drove it deep into the creature's skull.

More trumpeting. Not of fear anymore, but of pain.

Other thieves joined in. Many jumped onto the elephant that Nathan was on. Stephen and a few others leaped onto the other. Within minutes, both elephants were dead.

Nathan approached me as his raccoon crawled up on his shoulder. "Nice job."

"Nice job?" I questioned. "I just saved your life."

"Don't push it."

"Stephen!" A voice suddenly rang out. "Nathan! Stephen! Help, quick!"

Nathan's eyes grew huge.

"Isaiah!" Nathan and Stephen both shouted. They immediately took off after the voice.

"Help! Auugghhh!" The voice screamed.

"ISAIAH!" Stephen cried.

I ran after them.

NATHAN

Isaiah was in trouble. Stephen and I ran side by side, desperately trying to reach the boy.

"Help! Auugghhh!" Isaiah cried out.

"No!" I whispered. I ran faster. As fast as I could. However, Stephen was running twice my speed.

"ISAIAH!" Stephen yelled out.

We ran further to where we heard the scream.

Isaiah was on the ground.

With a massive gash in his chest.

Stephen and I dropped to his dying side. Stephen clutched his brother's hand and began stroking back his black hair.

"Stay with me, Isaiah." Stephen whispered soothingly.

"Stephen, I'm sorry." Isaiah cried. "He was getting away. I was going to stop him for you."

"Who was getting away?" Stephen was confused.

"The assassin." Isaiah coughed. "He was limping away. I was going to...I was going to stop..."

"Stop talking, Isaiah." Stephen ordered. Then he frantically glanced around at his lackeys. "Get Samuel! Is he still alive? Get him here now!"

"I'm so sorry, Stephen." He said again. He began fading.

"Isaiah, no." Stephen turned back to his brother. Stephen started talking faster. "Stay with me, Isaiah. Isaiah, Isaiah, brother. No."

Then...Isaiah passed away.

JONATHAN

I reached where Stephen and Nathan had run to. Sophia limped behind me. Stephen's little brother was dead. I immediately turned and shielded Sophia's eyes.

"Don't look, your highness." I instructed her.

She pushed my hand out of the way and stared at the boy.

"Princess." I said to her.

She ignored me. She simply stared at the boy.

"I…was just talking to him. He was…just there." She spoke softly. Her eyes were filled with shock.

"Sophia, please, look away." I told her. I knew how it was. Death was a horrible thing to witness.

"The assassin was after you." Stephen mumbled to Nathan. Stephen continued clutching the dead body of his younger brother. We all remained silent.

Nathan took a step closer to Stephen. "But, I...killed him."

"Oh, did you now?" Stephen's tone was dangerous.

"Stephen, he had swords in his chest and gut. There's no way-"

"My brother is dead!" Stephen stood, glaring wildly at Nathan. "That assassin is *not*!"

Nathan remained silent. He drew in a breath.

"I'm sorry, Stephen." Nathan said quietly.

Then without a moment's hesitation, Stephen tackled Nathan. Stephen was plowing fist after fist into Nathan's body as they rolled through the dirt. In the process, Nathan's raccoon fell off of Nathan's shoulder. Korhn looked like he was about to jump on Stephen, but Sophia grabbed him before he could.

"You ruined everything for me!" Stephen roared.

Suddenly, Nathan threw a punch into Stephen's jaw.

"Fool!" Nathan raged. "You did just as much damage as I did!"

"Liar! Liar!" Stephen shouted as they continued their brawl. I found it rather awkward. Here I was with Princess Sophia and forty bandits, watching two other bandits fight

"Jonathan, stop this!" Sophia ordered me.

I glanced around. Stephen's bandits weren't doing anything. I wondered what they would do if I suddenly barged in. However, most seemed too tired to do anything.

I sighed. "Yes, Princess Sophia."

I jumped in the fray. I grabbed Stephen's arms as Nathan finished beating him. Nathan knocked him down and gave him a few more punches. Stephen was done.

"You scum!" Stephen insulted. "I hate you!"

Nathan ran up and kicked Stephen once more. As he did, two of Stephen's men both knocked Nathan to the ground.

"The feeling's mutual!" Nathan shouted as he struggled to get back up.

"This isn't helping anything." I said to both of them.

"Jonathan is right." Sophia spoke up. "None of us are the true enemy."

At the same time, Stephen and Nathan's eyes flashed with realization.

"It's Mirrac." Sophia continued.

Stephen slowly picked himself up. "She's right."

Nathan remained silent.

Stephen had a hate in his eyes. "Iarrag Castle is under Mirracian control, isn't it?"

"Yes." Sophia responded.

"And the assassin that killed my brother is heading there?"

"I-I'm...not sure." Sophia confessed.

"Worth a shot." Stephen growled. "I'm going to Iarrag."

"To take it back?" I questioned him.

"No." Stephen told me. "To kill my brother's murderer."

"That's suicide." I informed him. "You'd die."

"I don't care." Stephen snapped. "My brother is dead. I'll avenge him or join him."

"I'll go too." Nathan said quietly.

Sophia turned a worried glance to him but said nothing. Stephen gave him a glare, but didn't say anything either.

"You two are going to take Iarrag?" I questioned. "Mirrac is the only one who's taken Iarrag in years."

Stephen glared at me. "Don't underestimate me."

Suddenly, Stephen began walking away from us. His men, which weren't many, followed without question. Nathan followed too.

"Sophia." He called over his shoulder.

"Yes?" Sophia asked.

"Watch Korhn for me."

CHAPTER EIGHT
ATTACK ON IARRAG

NATHAN

We were going to attack Iarrag.

Before Leos' attack, Stephen had over one hundred bandits under his command. Thirty-seven of them had survived Leos' attack.

Nearly seventy of Stephen's thieves had been killed. William would have been overjoyed.

Me included, thirty-nine bandits were going to attack a heavily fortified castle. Iarrag was under complete control of Mirrac. Hundreds of guards.

An insane, suicidal, foolish plan.

But we didn't care. Stephen was enraged at Isaiah's death. His followers were loyal to him.

Me?

My failure to end Leos cost Isaiah his life. Isaiah's death was on my hands.

And my tribe was still unavenged as long as Leos drew breath.

I wanted him dead.

Plus, if we succeeded, I would be keeping my word to Sophia. Safely back in Iarrag.

We hid out in the woods next to Iarrag. Stephen and I were at the head of our small band of thieves.

Stephen turned to me.

"This is only temporary." He glared. "After this, we're enemies again."

I sighed. "Stephen, I-"

"Understood?" Stephen interrupted.

I sunk a bit. "I just don't understand why we can't go back to how things were."

"You know darn well why!" Stephen growled.

I remained silent.

Stephen turned away from me, glancing back at Iarrag.

"You always were too soft, Nathan." He snarled. "And I'm going to kill you someday."

"Sounds lovely." I muttered angrily. "We should set a date. Send out invitations."

"Enough of this." Stephen snapped. "We have a job to do. Kill the Mirracians."

"June doesn't work for me. Too hot." I added.

Stephen ignored me and turned to his men. "My brothers. We are here to avenge Isaiah's death. Go to your positions, infiltrate Iarrag, and meet up in the dungeon. If any you don't make it that far, I wish you farewell."

I stepped forward. "None of you have to come with us. If anyone wants to leave, you can now."

Stephen's eyes flashed with rage, but he said nothing. I knew I had gone where I shouldn't have.

"We will fight with Stephen to the end." One thief replied. "We are his loyal servants. Where he goes, we follow."

The others nodded and grunted in agreement. I stepped back, letting Stephen know I was finished speaking.

His anger faded away, seeing that his men weren't going to listen to me.

"Move out." He ordered.

Instantly, the thirty-seven thieves all scattered and ran, in one way or another, towards Iarrag. I pulled up my mask and was about to run off with them as well, when Stephen grabbed my shoulder.

"Oh no." He said. "You're staying with me, Hieun."

I gulped. "Where is our area then?"

"We're going through the front gate." Stephen had a sinister smile. "You're going to be my catch."

Humiliation and panic.

Those were my feelings. Stephen had his sword at my throat and was dragging me towards the gates.

We had an…argument…about Stephen's plan.

"This won't work!" I told him. "You're a thief too! They'll kill us both!"

"No, they won't." Stephen replied calmly. "Seth wants you. They'll think that I came to collect payment for you. You have a bounty, don't you?"

"Like they know what I look like!" I shrieked.

Stephen removed my mask with a violent pull. "That assassin will know you."

"And if he's not here?!" I asked him.

"Then I guess I get my payment." Stephen chuckled. "I win either way."

"So much for forgiveness." I groaned.

"At least I'm not killing you." Stephen pointed out.

We reached the gate. Guards on top of the wall began to spot us. Stephen threw off my hood. He grabbed me by the hair and pulled. "What's the assassin's name?" He whispered.

"Stephen, this won't-!" I grunted through grit teeth.

"Give me the name!" He growled in a hush. He yanked on my hair again

"Leos." I winced.

"What is your business here?" A guard called down, addressing Stephen.

"I'm looking for Leos, sir." Stephen replied with a respectful tone. "I hear he's looking for this thief."

The guard gave him a questioned look. The guard then turned his gaze to me.

"Who is he?" The guard questioned Stephen.

"Nathan the Hieun, sir."

I saw recognition go through the guard's eyes. He knew my name. The guard spoke to another guard on the wall. After they finished, the second guard disappeared from view.

"He's going to go get Leos." I groaned. "You're going to get me killed."

"Only if you don't take this opportunity." Stephen informed me. "This is a sure-fire way to get you safely inside. And it will be a distraction for the rest of us. Scope out the castle and find weak points in their defenses. We need you for this."

I was shocked by this. Stephen was actually trusting in me with the most important role. Not only that, but he wasn't taking the chance with me getting caught by sneaking in. This was the safest way of getting on the inside.

…Either that or he was just telling me that so I would stop blubbering. Yeah, that was probably it.

Suddenly, Leos emerged on the top of the wall. It had only been a few hours since he had three swords stuck in him.

Yet, he looked perfectly fine.

He spotted us both and glared.

He was not happy.

"Where is the girl?" Leos growled.

Stephen tried to control the anger in his voice. He wasn't succeeding. "How should I know?" He snarled back. "I brought you Nathan."

Leos seemed to have some satisfaction with me captured. "Still expect payment, boy?"

Stephen took a breath. "No."

Leos smiled. "Then you've learned."

He suddenly tossed a sack to Stephen. Stephen released me and snatched the sack out of the air.

I immediately took off as soon as Stephen let go of me. I knew I probably wouldn't get away...

But it was worth a try.

Leos whistled. I heard something fly through the air.

"Fhht!" An arrow stuck through my boot and into the ground. I instantly tripped and tumbled in the dirt. As soon as I stopped rolling, I checked my foot.

Incredibly, the arrow had missed my foot. I sighed with relief.

"*That was really close.*" I noted as I glanced back at Stephen and Leos. Stephen had several coins in his hands, counting them. Leos was smirking at me. Guards were beginning to exit the gate, coming to collect me.

"Want to try running again, Iveslo?" Leos snickered. "*That* was a warning. Run again, the archer will shoot to kill."

So, I gave myself up. Stephen began walking away, smiling that he actually got paid.

And me? I was now being dragged into the city by guards.

"What should we do with him, sir?" A guard asked Leos.

Leos pondered on it, glaring at me.

"Sir?" The guard asked again.

"Tell me, Philip." Leos said to the guard. "Should I kill him, or hand him personally to Seth?"

Suddenly, I became very fearful.

"Sir?" Philip asked nervously.

"Should I kill him or present him to Seth?" Leos repeated.

"I, uhh, don't believe I can answer that, sir." Philip told Leos.

Leos glanced at him. Then glanced at me.

"I should kill him, shouldn't I?" Leos asked out loud.

I panicked. "No! Please no!"

Leos ignored my plea. He turned to the guard. "He's been causing me trouble all this time. It would be better just to give Seth his head."

"Leos, if you do, you'll be sorry!" I yelled at him.

That got his attention. "Really, Iveslo?"

He squatted down to my height. His face was full of disbelief. "And why would I be sorry?"

My mind went blank. "*Why **would** he be sorry?*"

I had no idea. I simply said it to try and save myself.

Leos kept his gaze at me. "Tell me, Iveslo. Why?"

I gulped. "Because…I know what Seth wants."

"You know what Seth wants?" Leos was still not believing me.

"You're a disappointment to him." I accused. "You're dead weight to him. He doesn't care about you and, when the time comes, he'll dispose of you."

Leos gave a chuckle. "You know what's funny? You're not wrong. But I know you'll say anything to save yourself. But right now, *I* really know what Seth wants. He wants *you* disposed of."

My mind raced furiously. "You're really going to kill me?! An innocent boy that was like a son to you?!"

His face was emotionless. "Yes."

"Why?" I shrieked, fear welling up inside me like an explosion.

"First, you are not innocent nor were you like a son to me." Leos pointed out. "And I'm very, very deep in Hieun blood, young Iveslo." For a moment, I saw sorrow in his countenance. I saw regret. Remorse. "I can't go back. I need to finish what I've started."

He stood up straight and began to walk away.

"Kill him." He ordered the guard. The guard lifted up his sword.

Fear, panic and anxiety instantly swelled up in my stomach.

"At least face me like a true Hieun!" I let out without a second thought.

Leos and the guard both froze.

"Or have you lost even that?" I challenged. "Be a man!"

Slowly, Leos turned to me.

The guard looked to him. "Sir?"

Leos took out his axe. "Free the boy."

I had no idea what I had gotten myself into, but before I had no chance of survival.

Now I had a chance. A very slim chance.

But I also had my chance to take my revenge against Leos.

I had vowed that I would kill him or die trying.

Now did those words truly ring in my head. Those were the options: Kill Leos or die.

I was brought to a large clearing. Guards were surrounding us, preventing any escape.

Leos had his axe. I was given a sword.

This was it.

Leos traditionally knelt to me and I knelt to him.

"Scyturaet-nogartuhe ipno byadutuliet, heojnoojra ipno daetadtuhe."

Leos spoke in Hieun.

"Scyturaet-nogartuhe ipno byadutuliet heojnoojra ipno daetadtuhe." I repeated. It was a tradition for us Hieuns. Before each challenge, the contenders would both kneel and say to each other "Strength in battle, honor in death" in Hieun.

Now the battle would begin.

I immediately charged at him. Leos waited for me, guard down.

He was taunting me.

That got me angry. I got close enough.

I swung the sword. A sharp clang rang out as it collided with Leos' axe.

He smirked. "Not fast enough. Not strong enough."

"You think I was trying?" I laughed. "I'm seeing if you're still hurt. Turns out, you're not wanting to move."

"Don't need to move." He told me. He shoved me back with his blade.

I nearly fell over with his small push. The man was strong.

But I could beat him with speed. I ran at him again.

This time he could see that I was ready. He put his guard up.

I ran at him, but slid past him and around him.

He was surprised at this. I was behind him and he sure wasn't able to turn around to block me.

I charged furiously at him, finally hoping to avenge my parents.

...I failed.

Leos stomped on my foot. A move I hadn't anticipated, and very effective.

"Gaaah!!" I shrieked.

Suddenly, overwhelming pain in my face. Leos had struck me in the nose.

I fell to the ground, bleeding and crying.

I opened my eyes to see Leos.

Axe!

I rolled out of the way, evading it by inches.

Leos was slower than usual. I leaped to my feet and backed out of his range. I wiped the tears from my eyes.

Leos laughed with his deep voice. "Pathetic! Utterly pathetic!"

"I've got a few fingers broken!" I shouted in excuse.

Leos laughed harder. "As I said. Pathetic."

I ran at him again. "I'll show you pathetic!"

Leos swung at me...and

...I jumped over him...

I never knew I could jump that high.

And while in the air, I flipped and sliced Leos across the shoulder.

"Ah!" He groaned.

I landed on the ground behind him.

"Whoa!" I let out before I could stop it.

I instantly spun to face him again, but he was ready for me.

"Gah!" I squeaked as his axe was flying at me again. I ducked and, again, rolled away out of Leos' reach.

Leos wasn't moving much, considering his wounds. He may not have been bleeding, but he was still hurt. I could move where he could not. I had a bit of an advantage. A very slim bit.

But in the end...it wasn't enough.

I was met with several strikes, slices, and insults of my parents.

I hated him. Oh, how I hated him.

I gave one final attempt with a swing of my sword...and my face met his foot.

I was smashed to the ground, bleeding, broken, beaten.

Leos stomped on my back.

I cried loudly for all the Mirracian guards to hear.

"Now you'll die, Iveslo." Leos whispered to me.

He raised his axe high up. I closed my eyes.

"Fhht!" A small whistle sounded.

A clang of armor hit the ground.

I opened my eyes.

A Mirracian soldier was dead with an arrow in his back. I searched around.

I spotted Stephen.

…With a small army.

Stephen and his thirty-seven thieves had released the prisoners of the dungeon and gathered the servants who were under Mirracian order. It was a multitude of Ferandarons. Guards, shop-keepers, commoners. Stephen pointed at Leos, who was shocked with unbelief.

"I want him." Stephen said quietly.

LEOS

"Kill them!" I roared at my men. A battle instantly erupted as Ferandarons and Mirracians collided in a huge brawl. I quickly turned back to Iveslo. The boy was trying to crawl away in an attempt to save himself.

I again stomped on him, crushing his leg under my boot. He let out a weeping yell. He was beyond fighting. He was beaten far too much to fight. But I didn't want him beaten. I didn't want him wounded.

I wanted him dead.

He **had** to be dead.

I knew I had to kill him

"*Fool!*" I cursed at myself. "*You should have just killed him! 'Honor'?! It was all just to delay me!*"

I lifted my axe, much hastier than before. I could hear men advancing behind me.

"*Kill him! Kill him!*" I raged.

"Help! Help!" Iveslo cried.

"*Too late, boy!*" I thought in satisfaction. I brought my axe down…

But I was stopped.

A man tackled into me, knocking me to the ground and saving Iveslo's life.

"NO!" I shouted in anger. I slammed the man's head into the stony ground and threw him off of me.

Iveslo was trying to get away again. Get to safety.

I charged at him, swinging my axe at anyone who came near.

A man with a spear

SWING!

Finished.

A woman with a sword.

SWING!

Next.

Two men with axes.

SWING!

Both down.

Then I reached my target. Iveslo.

SWING!

…a miss.

Iveslo was still fast, though he was crippled and broken.

"You're mine, wretch!" Stephen's voice sounded behind me.

I instinctively swung behind me. The boy dodged.

He lunged at me with a sword. An easy block and the sword was broken.

The boy was defenseless.

"I'm tired of you." I snarled.

"Stephen!" Others around me yelled and they swarmed me. They all began beating me and attempting to stab me.

I threw them off, swinging my axe wildly. I began slaughtering any who approached me. Man, woman, even Mirracian.

I didn't care.

I was in an absolute rage.

"*RAAAAAAAAAAAAAAAAAAAAAAAAAAAAHHHHH!!!*" I roared, blinded by the blood on my face. I swung at everything that I could see moving.

My speed was enduring, my strength was unmatched.

But I knew I could not take on an army by myself. For I could vaguely see that the other Mirracians were fleeing.

I was alone to battle the Ferandarons.

"*FLEE.*" The power inside me ordered. "*YOU MUST FLEE NOW. YOU ARE OUTNUMBERED. YOU WILL DIE.*"

There was no doubt in my mind that I wouldn't survive if I stayed to fight.

But I had one task.

Iveslo still lived.

I searched all around me to find him, but my vision was clouded with the blood of my enemies.

Then I spotted him!

He was crawling away. His blonde hair exposed him.

I charged through the overwhelming crowd that surrounded me. Many stabbed me, greatly wounding me, but I simply slashed through.

Then I was tackled from behind. I was dragged to the ground.

"ENOUGH!" I shouted. I took hold of my axe with both of my strong arms. I fought to my feet.

I then spun a full circle, taking out a massive amount of Ferandarons. Blood was everywhere and I had made enough room to get to Iveslo. But my vision was blurred and I had lost sight of him.

There! I saw his cloak!

"FLEE! FLEE NOW! YOU HAVE NO TIME!" The power told me. I glanced around at the massive throng around me, closing in. Though I had killed many, there were more.

But I had to finish Iveslo. I had to.

I still had him in my sights. I took out a knife and fired it at him.

It struck perfectly! A fatal wound! My mission was complete.

"YOU MUST FLEE!"

"Then give me strength!" I commanded aloud.

Instant power. Without hesitation, I lifted my arms and brought them to the stony ground.

The entire area shook with a huge tremor. The warriors around me fell to the ground.

There was my escape! I immediately ran! My body was wrecked with searing pain, seeing I had suffered so much damage. But still I ran.

I made it past the gate and out to the fields.

I whistled loudly for Saums. He came into view quickly after I called for him. He hadn't been very far from Iarrag. When he was within range, I nearly collapsed from the condition I was in.

"Get us…out of here!" I yelled breathlessly. "Iarrag is taken…but Iveslo…will die."

Saums's eyes glowed with relief that I had finally completed the mission. He let me mount up on him and we headed towards Mirrac.

It was over.

JONATHAN

"We should have gone with." Sophia told me as we prepared for bed.

"We wouldn't last." I said as I built up a fire. "How many warriors did they have? Forty? Against hundreds? They're dead by now."

"You don't know that." Sophia glared at me. "Nathan is a great warrior."

I snorted in response. "It doesn't matter how great a warrior he is, he'll be-"

I suddenly stopped and looked at Sophia. "Wait…Do…Do you care for him?"

Just by the tone she had in her voice made me realize that she possibly had feelings for Nathan.

Her face immediately flushed red. She attempted to hide her face behind Korhn's fur.

"N-no." She stammered timidly.

I sighed, shaking my head.

"You do. You actually care for this…this thief." I said in amazement. Her face grew redder. She used her staff to help her to her feet. The raccoon hopped off and sat next to the woodpile.

"I do not!" She argued defiantly. "He…He's just a…good friend. And stop calling him that."

"A thief?" I questioned. "He is one."

"He wasn't always." She folded her arms and turned away from me. "I've heard his story."

"Oh, really?" I mocked. "You just believed some sob story he told you? Sophia that's what they all do. They try to get you to feel sorry for them so they can trick you."

"You're wrong." Sophia said without hesitation. "He's different."

"How is he different?"

"I…I just know."

I realized another tone in her voice. "What are you hiding from me?"

"Nothing." She said quickly, still turned away from me. "I'm hiding nothing."

I feared the worst. "Sophia…did he…take advantage of you?"

She spun around. "Good gracious, of course not!"

"Then what are you not telling me?" I questioned her, staring into her eyes.

She toyed with her hair, as she usually did when she was nervous. Her face grew red again.

"We...danced." She spoke, smiling sheepishly.

"Now how in blazes can you say he's different from one dance?" I rolled my eyes.

"He is!" She stomped her good leg.

"How do you know?" I asked, annoyed.

She calmed herself a bit, seeming like she was remembering.

"I've danced with many men, Jonathan. You included."

I felt a wave of embarrassment come over me. "We were kids..."

She shushed me. "Let me finish."

I swallowed. "Yes, ma'am."

She sighed. "Out of every man I've danced with...I mean the ones that Father wanted me to consider for...courtship...I never wanted it. But with Nathan, there was no pressure. No one watching to see if we would 'be a good couple'. And it wasn't only that...Nathan *is* different. He's a thief, but he has morals. He's different from any prince that I've ever met."

I sighed, pinching the bridge of my nose. "Sophia...there's more to a relationship than dancing. And maybe he has some code, but let's face it, you don't know him."

I expected Sophia to argue or get discouraged at that. She didn't. Instead, she smiled sheepishly as a twinkle formed in her eyes. That worried me.

"You're right." She said dreamily. "So I want to get to know him more."

NATHAN

My leg was broken. I could still feel how Leos crushed it. Now I knew how Sophia felt...

Fortunately, I had safely found a hiding spot and stayed there until Leos had left.

I was still pondering on how he made the earth shake.

"That was beyond Human power." I thought. *"Where did he get that strength? Not to mention being able to take so much damage...That can't be possible."*

Apparently, it was.

Then again, taking a sword to the chest and two swords to the gut without dying was pretty impossible too.

"Leos must have discovered some dark power." I concluded. *"Demonic or witchcraft-y. That would explain some things."*

That was all the time I was able to think on Leos' strange abilities, because I was found by a Ferandaron spearman.

"You there!" He called when he spotted me hiding. "Who are you?! Mirracian?!"

"No, no!" I put up my hands, showing I had no weapon. "I was a prisoner!"

"He's one of us." Another voice called. The man that had saved my life earlier. He had tackled Leos and kept his axe from impaling me. He was short, but burly. He had very, very short brown hair on top of his head. He was wearing an apron. He held out his hand to help me up. I took it, but I needed more help to actually stand.

"I'm the baker." He told me.

The thought made me laugh. A baker, being able to fight like that? Hilarious.

Although, it did explain the apron.

I then recognized him.

"Oh, I remember you." I groaned. "I knocked over your bread..."

He smiled. "And I got you back for that, if you recall. I knocked you out when you broke into my house."

"And...then you turned me over to the Mirracians?" I questioned.

"Hey, don't get bitter." He laughed. "We're friends now. We weren't then. I'm Jason."

"Nathan!" A voice called. I saw one of Stephen's thieves run to me. "Come quick!"

Jason helped me over to where the thief was calling me.

We found Stephen with a knife deep in his back.

A fatal wound. I glanced at the knife that pierced him.

It was Leos'.

"Step aside!" a physician pushed past me. He checked Stephen as my rival groaned in pain.

"How is he?" Jason asked the physician.

The physician looked up from Stephen. "It will kill him. I can't help him."

I had mixed feelings. One part of me was grateful that I didn't have to deal with him anymore, seeing he was out to kill me and make me wish I was never born.

But the other…

Well, the other part was…in sorrow.

This person was my friend. Though we may have had a war between us, he was my friend.

And that greatly outweighed the relief I had.

"Is there any possible way we can save him?" I asked the physician desperately.

"The wound is too deep." The physician informed me. "He won't make it."

Stephen, excluding his cries of pain, was silent throughout this. He had a look of regret on his face.

"There has to be some way." I argued. "Isn't there anything?"

"None that I know of." The physician stated sadly.

"But we can't just give up so soon, I mean he-" I began to say.

"Let me die, Nathan." Stephen grunted softly, interrupting me. "I tried to avenge my brother and I failed. Let me die."

Those words ate at me. Let him die? Just like that? I knew what it was like to try and avenge a loved one and fail. Had it not been for Nila, so many years ago, I would've died by Leos' hand.

"There is a way we can help him." Jason suddenly spoke with realization. "I know a healer."

I turned to him. "Where?"

He frowned a bit. "She lives in Teshba. About three hours south of here."

"He'll only last a day, if we're lucky." The physician added.

"Okay." I said to Jason. "You get us some horses. Quickly."

He ran off towards the stable.

Then I turned back to the physician. "Help him up on one when Jason comes back."

The physician blinked at me. "You really believe this will work?"

"We've got to try." I told him. "I owe it to him."

In the corner of my eye, I saw Stephen look at me. I didn't know whether or not he would forgive me, but I knew that I had shown him that I had forgiven him.

Jason ran back with two horses.

"We don't need two." I told him. "Stephen may not be able to ride."

"I'm coming too." Jason explained. I didn't reject his help. The physician and some others helped Stephen up on one of the horses. I mounted up behind him. I was offered help, and I gladly accepted it. My leg was broken. Just sitting on that horse brought excruciating pain.

Jason got on his horse. I glanced around at all the Iarrag servants around me. Then I remembered Sophia and Jon.

"By the way." I cleared my throat. "Uh, the princess is hiding out in the woods not far from here. Someone...should, uh, probably go get her."

That was a pathetic speech.

The people's eyes immediately widened.

"The princess?!"

"Where is she? Is she safe?"

"What happened to her?!"

I was bombarded with hundreds of questions all at once.

"Hey, I just-no, she's fine. Listen, I wanted to-please just quiet down and I'll tell you. Would you just-" I tried to quiet them down.

I began to get frustrated.

"Hey!" I yelled out. "Just go get her! She's out there, about a couple miles northwest!"

The crowd quieted down a bit.

I turned to Jason and gestured toward the gate. "Lead the way."

"Hyah!" He urged his horse, running through the gate. I followed after him.

Stephen coughed weakly. "Nathan, why...are you doing this?"

"Because, contrary to what you think, we are not enemies." I told him. We rode out the gate just as the sun started to rise.

SOPHIA

I lazily teased Korhn with a blade of grass as the sun peaked over the horizon. Jonathan had gone hunting and returned with some sort of animal. He began cooking it for our breakfast.

"So what are we going to do?" I asked Jonathan as Korhn reached up for the blade of grass I had. I pulled it farther away, out of his reach.

"We do what your father did when he was younger." Jonathan pondered. "For now, we have to leave Ferandar. Cheqwa might be a good place to go."

"Cheqwa?" I shuddered. "Why not Oridion?"

"Oridion is already partly under Mirracian control." Jonathan reasoned. "Cheqwa hasn't been touched yet."

"Will that be far enough?" I asked. "Out of Mirrac's reach?"

"If it isn't, at least we stand more of a chance." Jonathan said grimly.

Suddenly, there was a sound of someone approaching. Jonathan stood up, unsheathing his sword. I turned to find that the sound was coming closer.

"*Nathan?*" I questioned.

Jonathan ran in front of me. He was ready to battle.

"Run, Princess." He ordered.

"Jonathan, it's probably just Nathan." I whispered to him. "…And I can't run."

Then, without warning, a shadow moved out of the darkness. It was lightning fast! Jonathan sliced at it but it easily maneuvered past him. I was tackled with an embrace.

"Princess! I'm so, SO glad you're safe!" Eila shrieked.

"Eila?" I gasped as I recognized my dear friend. Eila was one of my personal servants. She wore dark clothing from her neck all the way to her feet. She had long light brown hair that went down to her hips but she kept it in a long braid. She was one of my servants that was trained for combat. She had actually been trained to be an assassin by her parents before she became my servant. Stealth and speed were her specialty.

I embraced her back. "I've missed you so much!"

"And I've missed you, Princess Sophia!" Eila hugged me tight. Suddenly, she pulled away.

"Princess, you're filthy." She gasped. "And what are you dressed in?"

172

I examined myself. I hadn't taken a bath in several days and I had been out in the forest for the majority of the travel home. I hadn't changed or even washed the garments that I had traded for either.

It was rather putrefying. I was almost as filthy and had a stench as bad as Nathan.

I was immediately humiliated.

"I...Oh, I'm disgusting." I said, completely ashamed.

Then suddenly, I heard Diana, my other servant, call out.

"Eila, did you find her?" She questioned.

"She's over here!" Eila responded.

More rustling and Diana appeared from out of the brush with her bow in her hand. She had long black hair and had somewhat dark skin. Not as dark as a Gronkon, but not as white as a Ferandaron. An immediate smile came upon her face when she saw me.

Within seconds, she was embracing me as well. Jonathan watched as we all cried with joy and greeted each other again. Diana was also repulsed by my appearance, but her joy in seeing me overcame that.

Then Eila noticed my leg. "Princess, what happened to you?"

"It was crushed by a carriage." I told them. "But it's fine, it's only broken."

"And you've been walking on it?" Diana asked, shocked.

I gave a small smile.

"Dear princess!" Eila gasped. "Here, we'll carry you back to Iarrag where the physician can see you."

Suddenly, something came to my mind. *"Wait, was Iarrag taken back from Mirrac??"*

Jonathan was thinking the same thing. "Wait, is Iarrag under Ferandaron control again?"

"Yes, it is!" Diana beamed. "Mirrac fled after a group of thieves released us and we fought this huge brute."

"He just wouldn't die." Eila added. "He killed so many people. I don't know how he did it."

"Leos." I thought.

"So, Nathan and Stephen *actually* pulled it off?" Jonathan said in disbelief.

"Oh, yes!" I said in realization. "Was there a thief there?"

As soon as that came out of my mouth, I knew that was ***much*** too vague.

"Which one?" Diana and Eila said at the same time.

I shook my head. "Umm, no, was there one with silver eyes?"

Diana's face went blank and she shrugged. Eila scratched her head.

"I'm going to be honest, I wasn't exactly staring deeply into any of their eyes, Princess." Diana said frankly.

"Do you have anything else that will help identify him?" Eila questioned.

"Was there any bandit that stood out?" Jonathan spoke.

"A few." Diana noted. "The leader of them all. Black, greasy hair. He released us from the prisons. I think his name was Stephen."

"No, the one I'm talking about, his name is Nathan." I clarified.

"Oh!" Eila exclaimed. "Yes! The blonde-haired boy!"

My ears perked up. Nathan did have blonde hair, didn't he? His hood always veiled his face, but I caught glimpses.

Eila turned to Diana. "Remember? He was the one who was going to save that other thief! He had a broken leg. The one who told us where you were at, Princess."

"Oh, yes." Diana remembered.

He sent my own servants to find me? I couldn't help but smiling. But then I thought of something else.

"Why didn't he come himself?"

Then it occurred to me.

"'Once we get back to your castle, I'm dropping you off and going back to what I do best'." I quoted Nathan's words softly.

"What did you say, Princess?" Diana asked.

I became sad. Jonathan, Diana, and Eila could all see.

"What's the matter?" Eila asked.

"Jonathan, they probably need you back at Iarrag. You should go. We'll catch up." Diana suggested, sensing that I didn't want to speak in front of him.

Jonathan got the message, did a small bow to me, and left.

"Now what is it, your highness?" Eila asked.

I didn't really want to talk, but I guess it would help. "The boy…"

"What about him?"

I knew I had begun to blush again. I played with my hair, trying to find the right words.

I didn't have to. They both saw the answer in my face.

"Ohhh." Diana groaned, a little disgusted.

"Aww." Eila smiled big.

"No." Diana nudged Eila. "Not 'aww'. He's a thief."

"I think it's sweet." Eila folded her arms.

"Is it wrong?" I asked them. "Just tell me the truth. Is it wrong? He is a thief, but he has a good heart. I think if he stayed, maybe we could change him."

"Aww." Eila repeated. "Of course we could."

"No, that's a terrible way to think." Diana said honestly. "People rarely change, Princess."

"Don't be such a downer, Diana." Eila scolded.

"I'm being realistic." Diana replied. "But, if you want, I suppose you'll just talk to him when he gets back."

I frowned. "He won't come back if he left."

"Why do you say that?" Eila pondered.

"He told me so." I hung my head. "He said we shouldn't get close."

Both of my friends sympathized with me and tried comforting me. It made me smile. Yes, I did care a bit for Nathan, but other than that, there was nothing between us.

They carried me back to the castle and I was greeted by familiar faces and embraces all around.

I was home.

Then I realized something. I turned to Jonathan as the massive crowd surrounded me.

"Where are my parents?"

CHAPTER NINE
A HUMBLE REQUEST

NATHAN

The healer we were looking for lived in a small city. Teshba. It didn't even show up on many maps. Less than fifty people lived there. As soon as we arrived, Jason rushed Stephen to a small house within the city. I took my time, hobbling on my one good leg. By the time I reached the inside of the home, I found Stephen lying on his stomach upon a small bed. A rather pudgy, black haired woman was pressing one of her hands on Stephen's wound, while her other hand was slowly removing the knife. Her healing hand was emitting a soft, blue glow. Before my eyes, I could see Stephen's deep wound rapidly heal and vanish away. As this happened, Stephen began sighing in relief and actually fell asleep.

There was…an awkward pause for a very long time after that. Jason and I took turns looking back from Stephen, to the healer, and back. The healer, seeing Stephen was healed, turned back to us. It was as if she was waiting for us to say something or whatnot. As the silence continued, the healer seemed to feel as uncomfortable as Jason and I did.

"That's it?" I asked, unable to take the silence anymore.

"That's it." The healer responded with an awkward smile. She held out Leos' knife to us.

"So…do we owe you anything?" Jason asked her as he took the knife.

"No." She replied. "I don't charge. That'd be really mean, because I heal people almost every day."

"So your magic is pretty popular, huh?" I questioned.

"Oh, it's not magic." The healer corrected me. "I'm no witch or anything. I was given this ability by the Shepherd. It's a blessing from Him, and I use it to His glory."

I squinted at her. "Well, what's the difference between magic and that?"

"Magic is used for evil, glorifying one's self. This power is used for good, glorifying the Shepherd as I use it."

"Hm." I muttered.

"Would you like some help with that leg?" The healer asked me. I blinked. I had a broken leg. I had actually forgotten that I had a broken leg.

"Can you do my fingers too?"

SOPHIA

I sunk in my bathwater, deeply troubled. It had been about a day since I had returned home, and things were not looking good. Not only was Nathan gone without saying goodbye, but my parents were back in Mirrac. Jonathan had explained how they were ambushed after Nathan and I fell into the lake. Jonathan admitted in shame that he fled. My father usually had deserters flogged. Flogged badly. Then, forced to work as a slave for several years until they could prove that they were worthy to be freed from slavery.

If they could prove they were worthy.

But I was now the leader of Ferandar. I was the princess, I made the decisions.

I didn't want to. I was in no way ready for leading a Nation, but I did make one decision:

Jonathan was completely pardoned for what he had done.

"Princess?" Diana spoke through the door, interrupting my thoughts.

"Hmm?"

"Your friend's giant rat-"

"Raccoon." I corrected.

"Yeah, that." Diana continued. "What do we feed him?"

"He likes fruit." I told her.

"Can I feed him?" I heard Eila ask Diana. "He's really cute!"

"Please, be my guest." Diana said to Eila. Then, Diana spoke to me again. "Princess? Are you all right?"

"Yes, I'm fine." I replied. "Just...thinking."

What was I going to do? I had a Nation to lead. A war to fight. I wasn't experienced in this. I needed help.

I grumbled a bit.

Help was something I wasn't going to get. The only ones that were left at Iarrag were servants, townspeople, or guards. All the knights, military leaders, and people of great importance had been taken to Mirrac.

I was alone with a small army.

"Nathan, please come back." I mumbled to myself.

Foolish. Very foolish.

I don't know why, but I reasoned that Nathan would know what to do. If I could find him, he could tell me what to do. How to lead this small army.

No use. He wasn't coming back.

"Well, no use pouting about it." My logic told me. *"You can't turn to him, so turn to the One who can help you."*

I sat up a bit, nodding. Then I bowed my head.

"My great and glorious Shepherd." I prayed. "…As You can see, I'm a little out of my wits here. Ferandar is in trouble. My parents are being held captive by Mirrac and I don't know what to do. I need Your wisdom. That, or I need You to send someone with the wisdom to help us in this dire-"

"Princess?" Diana called again, interrupting my prayer.

I groaned inwardly, rather annoyed.

"I'm fine." I reassured her.

"Um, that boy you were speaking about?"

I quickly sat up. "What of him?"

"He's here."

For a moment, I sat absolutely still in my bathwater.

"Thank You." I whispered quietly to the Shepherd.

Men really just cannot fathom what a girl must go through to look her best. From the moment Diana told me of Nathan's return, a scene of panic and chaos erupted in my room. I frantically finished bathing, and speedily hobbled to my closet. I ripped through my wardrobe for something that was elegant, yet not too imposing. Something that said "beautiful" but not "authoritative". After questioning Diana and Eila on which dress I should wear, which required me to put on nearly all of them, we came down to three choices:

1. A simple pink dress that reached to my ankles.
2. A fancier sapphire dress, arrayed in a few gems, that had a bit of a train.
3. A light green dress that was given to me as a gift from a prince in Oridion. It came with a delightful scarf.

Though it took some time and debating, the pink dress was deemed best. Nathan was not interested in fancy (unless he could steal it. Diana

179

had mentioned that with a smirk), and I honestly didn't like the green dress too much. The scarf was nice, however.

Once I knew what I was wearing, all I had left was to make sure my hair wasn't a nightmare and that my face didn't look like I had just been hibernating for an entire winter. That took an extra twenty minutes.

After all of that diligent work, Diana and Eila helped me make my way to the stables where Nathan and Jonathan were waiting…

And Nathan barely even noticed I was there.

I have to admit, I was deeply depressed in that moment. I went through *so much* for him, and he had no appreciation for it.

Men.

"Calm down. Calm down." I tried to make myself relax. *"He's not use to my kind of life. Plus, he's seen you when you were filthy and in peasant clothes. It just shows that he doesn't care about the outside. If anything, he looks on the inside, right?"*

"You look lovely, your highness." Jonathan said kindly.

My mood turned slightly sour again. Of course *Jonathan* noticed.

"Thanks." I replied with a somewhat aggravated tone. But there was no time to be bitter about who did and did not notice my efforts. I needed to focus on what was at hand.

I took in a deep breath as I acknowledged Nathan. "You came back."

"I did." Nathan nodded. "Though your knight here wasn't so warm in his welcoming."

Jonathan grumbled in response.

"What happened to Stephen?" I asked.

"He'll be fine." Nathan assured me. "The healer saved his life and he fell asleep. That's when I left. I'm not so sure he would want to wake up with me still there."

"You left a very dangerous criminal with a harmless healer?" Jonathan scolded. "How could you do that?"

"Don't worry, Stephen won't hurt her." Nathan assured Jonathan. "He is a thief, but he's not a monster. She saved his life. He won't hurt her or rob her. If anything, he'll owe her."

"In my experience, thieves don't have honor." Jonathan retaliated.

"Stephen does." Nathan glared. He stepped up to Jonathan, his silver eyes piercing at him. "Not all of us are heartless."

Jonathan didn't back down from him. He stared back, not letting Nathan push him back.

I felt uncomfortable. It was almost as if I had just completely disappeared. And the worst thing was that I didn't know what to do. They were just glaring at each other. Was a fight going to break out? "*Should I cough?*" I thought to myself. "*Let them know I'm still here?*" Thankfully, I didn't have to. Jason was exiting the stables, having returned the horses he and Nathan rode.

He was hauling a saddle away when he took one look at Jonathan and Nathan.

"You two going to stare-down all day?" Jason laughed at both of them. Nathan and Jonathan both turned their attention to the friendly baker.

"You two are funny." Jason grinned as he walked off with the saddle. With that, Nathan and Jonathan sat in silence for a couple seconds as we all watched Jason walk away.

"I continually get humbled by that man." Nathan clicked his tongue.

"He is a puzzle." Jonathan nodded. Then he glanced at Nathan. "Didn't Eila say you broke your leg?"

"Yes, but I did visit a healer." Nathan answered.

"Good thinking."

Nathan patted his leg with a smile as he turned to me. "Sophia, you ought to go see her."

"You said you wouldn't come back." I took the opportunity to get straight to the point, since my existence was being acknowledged again. "Why did you?"

That surprised Nathan. He took a second to think.

"Two reasons."

"Oh? Do tell."

"First, I wanted to make sure you were home safe and sound." Nathan explained. "Make sure I held up my part of the deal. And secondly…"

Suddenly, he whistled. Korhn, who was being held by Eila, jumped free, ran up Nathan's arm, and perched himself on Nathan's shoulder.

"I also needed this little guy back." Nathan scratched Korhn's ear. "Now that my job is done, and my head is clear of your father's sword, I'll be heading off."

But before he did, Nathan looked at me. He took a moment to…really look at me. His eyes were fixed on my eyes.

I'm not sure what he saw. I was thinking and feeling a terrible amount of things all at once.

All I know is that Nathan got something from that moment of looking into my eyes.

He let out a troubled breath. "But…you don't want me heading off yet, do you?"

I swallowed. "Not quite. I would like to ask you something."

Nathan waited patiently as I paused.

"I need your help." I confessed. "We all do."

"I don't." Jonathan muttered under his breath.

I ignored him. Thankfully, Nathan did too.

"I don't know what to do." I began to shuffle nervously. "My parents are in Mirrac. So are the military leaders. Ferandar turns to me for leadership. Admittedly, I can't give my people the leadership they need. We're in a time of war and desperation. I'm just a fifteen year old girl."

"You're not asking *me* to help you lead a Nation, are you?" Nathan asked, horrified at the idea.

"Ha!" Jonathan guffawed. "We'd be better off surrendering to Mirrac!"

Nathan's worry vanished and was replaced with scorn as he looked at Jonathan. Jonathan, still smiling, was looking to me, Diana, and Eila for supported laughter.

There was none. Instead, there was a nasty glare coming from me. Jonathan took the message, cleared his throat, and remained quiet.

"No." I returned my attention to Nathan.

"Well, I can't say I'm not relieved." Nathan said, giving Jonathan an annoyed glance before giving me his full attention. "So what are you asking of me?

At that instant, all eyes were on me.

Nathan's.

Jonathan's.

Diana's.

Eila's.

Even Korhn's.

I mustered up my courage and determination before stating my request.

"I want you to take me back to Lasónay." I said firmly. "And I want you to help us free my parents."

THE END OF BOOK ONE
THE ZALIAN CHRONICLES: VOLUME III

ABOUT THE AUTHOR

Nicholas M. Krohn has always had a love for both writing and the Lord. Nicholas received Jesus Christ as his Lord and Saviour at the age of nine, thanks to his faith-filled mother and a godly church. After his salvation, Nicholas spent most of his childhood free time jotting down fantastical stories that had a deep sense of Christianity within them. When he was a teenager, Nicholas discovered that writing was his calling from God. When attending Heartland Baptist Bible College, Nicholas began seriously writing and self-publishing novels with the desire that they would both wholesomely entertain readers, yet bring glory to God's name. It was here that he met his wife, Marissa, whom he married in 2017. Halfway through college, Nicholas also realized that he could do more than just write Christian Fiction. After deep study in the Bible and graduating from Heartland Baptist Bible College in 2020, Nicholas made it his mission to not only point to the Lord with his fiction novels, but to expound on the Word of God itself through commentaries, in-depth studies, and other such works of literature. Nicholas continues to pursue this work while living in Iowa with his wife and daughter.

OTHER WORKS OF THE KROHN FAMILY

MARISSA KROHN

The Silent Princess (*Children's book*)

NICHOLAS M. KROHN

BIBLE COMMENTARY SERIES

Krohn's Commentary of the First Book of Samuel

THE SCOEFIELD SERIES (*HISTORICAL FICTION*)

Scoefield

Engel

Made in the USA
Las Vegas, NV
04 May 2023

71549540R00111